D1525634

ACCLAIM FOR AWARI
BARRY FINLAY

## REMOTE ACCESS:
### *AN INTERNATIONAL POLITICAL THRILLER*

"Finlay paints a frighteningly realistic picture of two of the things people often fear today — terrorism and cybercrime."

– RECOMMENDED by the US Review of Books

"While grounded in reality, Remote Access is a must-read with a singular sense of escapism rare in a political thriller."

– BestThrillers.com

## A PERILOUS QUESTION:
### *AN INTERNTERNATIONAL THRILLER AND*
### *CRIME NOVEL*

"Written with a compassionate, knowledgeable voice, the book is an excellent story of mystery and intrigue."

– RECOMMENDED by the US Review of Books

"A Perilous Question sizzles with international intrigue as the tension and suspense mount to a compelling pitch. Barry Finlay will keep you turning the pages."

– Rick Mofina, Bestselling Author of *FREE FALL*.

## THE VANISHING WIFE:
### *AN ACTION-PACKED CRIME THRILLER*

"I had a hard time not just giving up the rest of my life and reading this in one sitting."

– Vaughan Hopkins, Amazon reviewer

"The pace grabs hold. Whether the mild-mannered accountant Mason Seaforth could actually pull off what's at stake depends on the colour, the energy and dialogue of the story telling. The Vanishing Wife is convincing."

– Donald Graves, Canadian Crime Reviews

## KILIMANJARO AND BEYOND:
### *A LIFE-CHANGING JOURNEY*

"The book reads like a journal and the writing is warm, familiar and humorous. 'Kilimanjaro and Beyond, A Life-Changing Journey,' will challenge all who read it to consider how they too can make a difference, not only for others, but for themselves as well."

– Reader Views

"...at once so inspirational and courageous, so human and humane, and so deeply personal that the reader feels they are climbing right along with this small and highly determined group."

– Reverend Dr. Linda De Coff, Author, Bridge of the Gods

# I GUESS WE MISSED THE BOAT:
## *A TRAVEL MEMOIR*

"This is an exhilarating read."

-– **Grady Harp, Amazon Hall of Fame reviewer**

"I Guess We Missed the Boat is a fresh, ironic and jovial travel adventure novel in which each traveler can recognize himself or herself. It is a travel book that is amusing and practical at the same time."

– **Reader Views**

# NEVER SO ALONE

# A NATHAN HARRIS THRILLER NOVELLA

BARRY FINLAY

# NEVER SO ALONE

An International Crime Thriller

Published by Keep On Climbing Publishing

Cataloguing data available at Library and Archives Canada.

ISBN: 978-0-9959379-5-6

# PREFACE

Fans of the *Marcie Kane Thriller Collection* will know that FBI Special Agent Nathan Harris was introduced in Book 2 - *A Perilous Question* and had an integral role to play in Book 3 - *Remote Access*. This novella, *Never So Alone*, takes the reader back in time before Nathan came into Marcie's life. The story begins in a fictional small town in rural Manitoba, Canada and continues to a city in the U.S. While the story is fictional, I relied on the expertise of some subject matter experts for accuracy where it was required. I would like to sincerely thank my nephew, Doug Finlay, Firefighter/Paramedic of the Rapid City, Manitoba Fire Department, for his knowledge and experience regarding volunteer fire departments. Volunteers of all types are dedicated people, but I think they have to be extra special to want to put themselves at risk fighting fires. A sincere thank you also to my sister-in-law, Marilyn Simpson and her husband Harvey, retired farmers in Roblin, Manitoba, who ensured my descriptions of farm life were accurate. Farmers are the backbone of society and are never given the credit they deserve so I hope, in some small way, I have honored their contribution in this novella. I'm very grateful to Doug, Marilyn and Harv for taking the time to read the story and provide feedback. Any liberties I have taken with the descriptions in the story are on me. A big thank you to Mirna Gilman at Books Go Social for the cover design. I'm also very appreciative of my launch team for their extra sets of eyes and for helping to get the book in the hands of the reading public. You are too numerous to mention, but you know who you are. Of course, my wife Evelyn is always the first to read and critique my work and I'm forever grateful for her support and enthusiasm.

Now, on to *Never So Alone*.

# CHAPTER ONE

Nathan Harris sat on a stool in the desolate barn contemplating the dust motes swirling in the air. Faint rustling nearby suggested a mouse with which he shared the space was scurrying back to its nest. It had probably carried out another raid of the peanut butter from a trap someone set. It must be a constant battle in the old building, he thought. The fall sunlight shimmered through the gaps in the boards, but a distant rumble announced a storm brewing in the west.

He was waiting on a farm located a few miles north of a picturesque little town on the Canadian prairies called Cedar Valley, in the province of Manitoba. The case assigned to him had produced zero results to date, but it appeared a break was imminent.

Maybe he could resume a normal life in the next few days, depending on how things transpired. He thought of Naomi. They had dated for more than a year and he thought she might be the one. But then before leaving, he saw a side of her he hadn't ever seen and it raised doubts. He felt horrible he couldn't tell her where he was going and she hadn't reacted well. He wasn't sure he wanted to bring her into his current life or whether she wanted to be included.

A man who worked the farm had dropped Harris off an hour earlier. When the organization rented the land and buildings, they leased large equipment and grew crops so it wouldn't surprise people living on the surrounding farms to see grain trucks come and go. Long-time employees of the organization farmed the land. The farming enterprise wasn't bigger or smaller than any other so as not to attract attention.

After the driver left, the only vehicle remaining in the yard was a loaded grain truck parked beside a bin. It was the last load scheduled to leave from this location and Nathan's job, as soon as he got a call giving him the go ahead, was to drive the truck across the border into the U.S.

The phone sat silently on a barrel beside him. When it rang he would know at last the American destination of the product he helped to manufacture for the last month. Since Canadian farmers can sell their wheat into the U.S. without restriction, the grain truck was a good cover. He had the paperwork in case the border guards asked questions.

Now he worried the people he worked with were watching him. *Had they discovered his identity?* He had to stay vigilant. If they wanted to send someone with him in the truck, he planned to insist he drive it across the border alone. He would also check his side mirrors often to make sure he wasn't being followed.

The sound of a vehicle's car tires crunching on the gravel lane leading to the buildings caught his ear. *That's odd.* He thought he was just going to be getting a phone call. Could be the neighbors dropping off an apple pie. *They do those things around here.* They would notice the grain truck in the yard and go to the house. To be sure, he walked to the front of the building to head the person off if they walked towards his location.

A door slammed. Nathan realized the car stopped a distance from the barn when a muffled male voice announced, "You wait here. I'll be right back." Peering through a crack in the wall, Nathan instantly knew the person approaching wasn't a neighbor. He had seen him at the barn a few times. His sixth sense told him something wasn't right. He moved further back into the shadows and reached behind his back for the comfort of the Smith and Wesson 5946 the RCMP provided him. His hand closed on the handle, ready to pull it out and fire at a moment's notice.

The sound of the man's steps increased as he neared the barn. Nathan weighed his options. Metal and plastic containers and copper pipe replacing the stalls at the back of the structure offered lots of places to hide. Rushing deeper into the back past the paraphernalia, he wondered how this would unfold. He resumed his position in the shadows and waited, thinking it would probably end badly for somebody.

The door, in need of a few drops of oil, screeched aside, brightening the interior with sunlight. A man of Nathan's size stood in the doorway, his frame outlined by the light behind him. He wore a baseball hat and had his hands buried in his bomber jacket pockets. He called out, "Penner, you here?"

Nathan pulled his gun from the waistband of his jeans and acknowledged the alias given to him when he started this assignment. "Yeah, I'm moving stuff around in the back, preparing for the tear-down next week. What are you doing here? I was expecting a phone call."

The man advanced from the doorway towards the center of the barn. He didn't say another word, just pulled something from his pocket and tossed it at a vat full of chemicals. Nathan rose from his crouched position and saw the man turn to sprint for the door. Nathan managed two steps forward before the shock wave lifted him off his feet and propelled his 200 pound frame backwards as if it was a paper napkin. It seemed like minutes before his body landed, but the seconds allowed time enough for several sensations to register. It was as if a catapult had flung a massive boulder into his midsection from a few feet away. An excruciating and sudden pain penetrated his ear drums as though someone jammed needles into them. His eyes registered a brilliant flash as if the storm had arrived and landed a lightning strike right at his feet.

The other thing that registered in his brain before everything turned to black was the debris raining down on him and how strange it was he couldn't hear it.

# CHAPTER TWO

The explosion rattled windows throughout the town of Cedar Valley and sound waves rocketed back and forth across the river. A flock of sparrows rose above the town as one from a tangled brush by the water, frightened by the ferociousness of the blast. Conversation ceased in the Now's The Time café as if a stranger entered the noisy room. The farmers and townspeople gathering at their regular time to discuss the harvest and share gossip about who did what to whom looked at each other in stunned silence. They came for a coffee and a piece of owner Clara's famous cherry pie and this was totally unexpected. Coffee and tea cups hung stranded in mid-air and mouths gaped in uncompleted sentences.

As the blast's reverberation faded into the distance, cups clattered back to the table and the conversation resumed. Everyone chattered at once. "Sounds like the pipeline blew up again," said one. "Sounded like it was north of here. Couldn't be the pipeline," said another. "Might have been Derek's gas barbecue." The speaker cast a toothless grin from under his bedraggled John Deere ball cap at Derek Barnsdale who responded by unwinding his middle finger with an imaginary crank. Barnsdale became the talk of the town the previous summer when he removed his eyebrows while using lighter fluid and a match to start his barbecue. The resulting fire melted a section of vinyl siding on his house.

Some rushed to the windows to push the drapes aside, looking for smoke. Others headed for the door. One of those was Ken Barber who, at the sound of the blast, set his cup on the checkered tablecloth, scraped his wooden chair back and rose to leave. Now in his late fifties, Barber was tall and reed thin. His wife had died of cancer a few years prior and his diet had suffered. He wore jeans and a wrinkled plaid shirt. An oversized ornamental bronze buckle with a 3D charging bull kept his belt cinched and his pants anchored around his waist. He pushed through the group standing in the doorway and counted in his head. Sudden trepidation enveloped him as a cloud of smoke billowing into the sky north of town rewarded the onlookers.

As Barber hustled along the street, his arthritic knee throbbing, he was sure it was a matter of time until he got a call. Known as the go-to odd-job man around town, he earned enough to pay for his needs. His parents and grandparents had lived in Cedar Valley and he had gone to the local elementary school until it closed. He taught himself everything about the intricacies of carpentry, electrical and plumbing, but as a result he could never get a job in the city. No certificate confirming his qualifications. He overcame his bitterness, and the townspeople loved his work ethic, ability and reasonable rates. An old hockey injury and bending and kneeling to do his work took its toll on his knee and it protested now. He wondered if approaching rain magnified the pain.

His destination was the local fire hall. The town named Barber the Chief of the volunteer fire department and he became a qualified first responder. The job kept him busier than he would have liked, often responding to brush and chimney fires and car accidents. He hated the latter because often the victims were people he grew up with or even worse, their kids.

The Cedar Valley volunteers who gave up their time from family and work trained to handle all situations like any paid firefighter. Barber hoped the explosion was explainable and his group wouldn't need to switch into fireman mode, but the thickening cloud of dark gray smoke drifting on the wind towards town told him otherwise. He needed to be at the station just in case. He cut through the general store's property and was approaching his destination when his pager and cell phone both vibrated. The count in his head stopped at a minute and 37 seconds.

Dispatch in the nearby city of Brandon sent out the message and announced on both devices that a caller reported an explosion and provided the name "Decker." The message also provided the section, township and range, the Canadian location co-ordinates where it had happened. He blew air through his nose thinking, I guess I *knew* it was an *explosion*. The old Decker place. His memory failed him as to how long, but the farm was in the Decker name for over a century. The old man died years ago, leaving disinterested kids behind. They hung onto it though and rented it to somebody about a year ago. He didn't know who. The townspeople discussed it many times over coffee at the restaurant, but other than seeing the new renters working the fields, they remained a mystery.

Barber unlocked the door and flicked on the station's overhead lights, illuminating the gleaming four trucks waiting to jump into action. It was the largest building in town and the firemen were proud of their fleet that serviced the surrounding area. The vehicles ranged in age from the late 90s to the early 2000s, but the proud volunteers and their spouses maintained them and kept them sparkling. Barber had his choice of trucks since he was the first one there. He decided on the tanker since the weight of its 1800 gallon capacity of water made it slower than the others.

He knew the other 15 members of the fire department would have received the same messages he did. They may not all show up, but he hoped almost everyone would today. He grabbed his fireman's gear off the hanger and hopped on one leg as he pulled the coveralls over his boots. The shock wave through his knee was agony. He groaned as he pulled himself into the tanker truck and settled behind the wheel. By pressing a single digit on his phone, he speed-dialed Wes and Nathalie Clermont, a husband and wife team of volunteers who lived in town, and asked them to bring the pumper truck and the rescue unit. Two of his next calls went unanswered, but he reached the next most senior volunteer, Adam Turnbull, and asked him to bring the rapid response vehicle. It was a smaller version of the pumper truck, but by the smoke rising from the property, they would require everything for this job.

He fired up the Ford tanker and hit the remote to lift the

double-wide door. Sunshine poured into the building as the door rose. Barber put the tanker in gear and coaxed the big truck out onto the street just as Wes and Nathalie Clermont turned the corner through the gaping doorway and hurried to find their gear on the hangers. Barber picked up speed as he thumbed the switch to start the siren wailing, hit the clutch and shifted into second while roaring through one of the town's few stop signs. Despite the siren and engine noise, darkening clouds approaching from the west produced distant thunder that rumbled through his open window. It explained his knee pain, but it was an unneeded reminder of the explosion that occurred only minutes earlier.

He wondered what new horror he and his team would find on this call.

# CHAPTER THREE

The lumbering tanker left the town limits and dropped off the pavement onto the gravel road that would take Barber to the Decker place. As he drove, he reflected on the quaint little town of Cedar Valley nestled between two ridges alongside the Timaskami River. It was close enough to, and yet far enough away from the city of Brandon in rural Manitoba, Canada, that the population never changed. Stately grain elevators, which once attracted farmers from near and far, disappeared long ago and the train now only rumbled through once a week. The bank met the same fate years earlier. Still, young people wanting the serenity of country living, while enjoying an easy commute to a desk job in the city, replaced residents who died. The town's population had hovered around 520 people for decades.

Cedar Valley came by its name honestly. Evergreens called Eastern cedars rose majestically in forested areas throughout the valley. The town hosted a skating rink, grocery store, the fire station, one gas pump, a nine-hole golf course, the ever-popular

Now's The Time café, and little else, but the people living there wouldn't think of moving. It suited them as they lived away from the noise and overcrowding of the city and enjoyed lower housing costs and property taxes. The commuters just had to avoid the deer and navigate icy road conditions in winter during their daily drive.

Barber always marveled at the willingness of the townspeople to get involved. They kept the town looking bright and homey and he was proud of his volunteer firemen. Residents of other small towns in the area envied their fleet of trucks. It took wheeling and dealing to get them. They were hand-me-downs from other more modern jurisdictions. The department purchased some at a very reasonable price and others were donated.

Dennis Jacks' bright yellow combine worked in the field at the crest of the hill just outside town. His field was about half done as the combine, nearly obscured by dust, spewed straw out the back to join the already harvested rows. Jacks seemed oblivious to the commotion going on around him, but Barber thought he was concentrating on completing the field before the rain came. Clouds threatened at other times this summer, but produced nothing. This time, by the look of the white streaks punctuating the fast-moving dark clouds, it looked like rain was imminent and Jacks would finish his work another day.

Barber's side mirror reflected the trucks driven by the Clermont's through the dust. The bright blue sky of minutes ago faded under assault from two fronts: the approaching storm from the west and the smoke billowing above the Decker's property.

The leaping flames against the somber gray sky beckoned Barber onward. Intermittent brilliant flashes of lightning spotlighted the Decker farm as the eerie darkness settled in. The combination weirdly reminded Barber of the cheap strobe lights bands used at dances in his teen years.

He rounded the last corner of the road heading to the Decker's just as the clouds swallowed the remaining sunshine. The sun's final farewell cast a flash of light from a metal surface that caught Barber's eye. It appeared to come from the end of Decker's lane.

An old rusty beige sedan barreled down the road directly at Barber's tanker. He pulled onto the soft shoulder to avoid being sideswiped. The soft gravel grabbed the right front tire and dragged the awkward vehicle towards the steep incline of the ditch as if it was quicksand. The truck would roll if the wheels dropped off the edge.

He realized in his haste he hadn't done up his seatbelt. Barber fumbled with the belt while yanking hard on the steering wheel and pumping the accelerator. The tanker tiptoed along the edge of the ditch with the right wheels now close to toppling over. He felt the truck respond and breathed a sigh of relief as he guided it back onto the road at the moment his seat belt clicked into place.

His heart thundering in his chest, he picked up the radio transmitter to call the drivers of the other vehicles. He checked the side mirror, but the dust clouds raised by the car and the three trucks obliterated any chance of seeing a license plate. It looked like the Clermonts had seen what happened as they had pulled over. "Dammit!" Barber muttered under his breath. *Did the car come from the Decker place?* Barber wasn't positive, but it sure looked like it had.

He checked the frequency on the radio to ensure the Clermonts, Turnbull and anyone in the station heard him when he spoke. His voice came out louder than intended when he pressed the talk button on the mike. "Some idiot driving a car that appeared to come from the Decker's almost ran me off the road. It's an old beige sedan." He twisted his neck to see over his shoulder that Turnbull had already left the outskirts of town and was shepherding the rapid response truck up the road at full speed. "Did anyone get a license plate number?"

Nathalie Clermont responded first from the rescue truck, "I pulled to the side when I saw him heading for you. There's so much dust, I couldn't see the plate." Her husband Wes in the pumper chimed in, "Same with me. I don't know what he was trying to do. He was driving like a maniac."

Adam Turnbull's shaky voice came through Barber's speakers. "He aimed right at me before he swerved at the last second. I have to admit I was like a deer in the headlights. The last thing I was thinking of was checking his plate. I'm just glad to be alive."

Barber neared the Decker's driveway, so he said, "No-one's responding from the station so they must all be on their way here. I'll call it in when we get stopped."

Barber's eyes widened as he turned the truck into the lane

leading to the Decker's. Total devastation. A pile of flaming rubble replaced the barn. He liked the Decker family and socialized with them before the old man died and the kids left town so the property was familiar. Now it looked nothing like he remembered. Ragged sections that used to be the front of the building rose through the smoke and flames, the rest having collapsed outward. The door lay in the yard about 30 feet away. The windows in the nearby house had either shattered or blown out completely. A piece of 2 X 4 extended like a huge nail driven part way into the trunk of a sizable tree that shaded the house for close to a century. An old shed, forced to lean a little further east each time a strong wind blew from the opposite direction, had succumbed to the blast.

Flames leapt from the front of the rubble and pieces of shattered wood burned in various areas of the yard where they landed. A grass fire flared up and the crackling flames growing in strength were in danger of engulfing the house. Barber assessed where to position the volunteers speeding to the property in their vehicles. He focused on the flaming pile that remained of the barn. As Nathalie and Wes Clermont descended from their vehicles, Barber directed them to hook the pumper to the tanker and aim the hose at the barn. When Turnbull arrived with the rapid response truck, Barber told him to take care of the grass fire before the tinder-dry vegetation erupted into something uncontrollable.

He dialed the Royal Canadian Mounted Police to report the car that aimed at his team like a guided missile and he wondered what caused a detonation of such magnitude.

The smell lingering in the air gave him an unwanted clue.

# CHAPTER FOUR

Lightning ripped apart the sky as the storm settled in overhead. Thunder echoed seconds after each flash, a warning that the storm hovered right on top of them now. The RCMP officer's voice disappeared with the rolling thunder so Barber grasped the door handle of the tanker and stepped on the running board to climb in so he could hear. A second whiff of the strange odor hit him as he put his foot on the step of the truck.

He hesitated. The stench was familiar. Recent training had brought it to his attention. Barber ripped a mask from a hanger and stepped down with the phone pressed against his chest. He half ran and half hopped toward Wes Clermont who dragged the fire hose towards the burning structure. "Wait! Stop! Get your masks and don't go too close!"

His words were unintelligible to the Clermonts, but the tone stopped Wes and Nathalie in their tracks just as the skies opened. It didn't just rain anymore. It either didn't rain at all, which was most of the time, or it came down in torrents. Mother Nature offered no in between this year.

"What's up?" Wes tried to make himself heard through the rain.

Barber caught up to them and gestured to the pumper. "Get your breathing apparatus and stay well back from the fire. I think I recognize that stink."

The intense heat from the crackling flames while they stood in the pouring rain offered a strange juxtaposition. Drops splattered off Nathalie's helmet as she turned back towards the pumper. She peered with her nose upturned to see past the water wriggling down the lenses of her glasses and dripping off the frames. "Smells like cat urine to me. Are you smelling something else, Ken?"

"Yes, it smells like either that or rotten eggs. Before the rain started, I also smelled a chemical odor. They're indications this could have been a meth lab." His training had taught him that meth labs are time bombs waiting for a spark to set them off and a byproduct is often strong chemical smells and unusual odors. If it turned out to be a lab, it would be Barber's first and, he hoped, last. He didn't want to risk any mistakes. "There could be more flare-ups. We have to stay well back and preserve it as a crime scene." They could drain the tanker in a few minutes so he was thankful the skies were co-operating. It was too time consuming to haul water to replenish the supply. "The rain will slow the fires."

The Clermonts collected their breathing apparatus while Barber finished his call and limped to Turnbull's location to share his theory about the lab. Other volunteers gathered around the pumper to receive a short briefing from the Clermonts.

The torrential rain helped the volunteers put out the fires without incident. They tried to preserve the scene while going only close enough to carry out their responsibilities. Barber reported the beige car to the RCMP and summoned the Fire Commissioner from Brandon by phone. Their conversation was brief.

The Commissioner asked what they had and Barber answered, "There was a major explosion. As soon as we arrived, I smelled something odd, like chemicals and cat urine or rotten eggs. I don't think it would be a propane tank rupture in the barn, but I wouldn't rule it out either. The odor has me worried. It has settled down thanks to the rain, but you need to examine the scene."

"Okay, I'll be there soon."

"There's one other thing. Someone tried to run us off the road on our way to the scene. I called it in to the RCMP. He nearly sideswiped my truck and ran me into the ditch. My man who was driving the rapid response truck, Turnbull, said the guy drove right at him and swerved at the last second. I'm not positive, but it looked like he drove away from the scene."

"What did the RCMP say?"

"They seemed extra concerned. They were sending a man from their closest detachment and putting out a lookout bulletin for the car. We didn't get a license plate; he drove past in a hurry, but it was a rusty beige sedan. I don't think he would get far before the RCMP got him."

"Okay, good work. I'll see you soon."

"I'll be here, sir."

Barber hung up the phone and sat in the warm confines of the tanker, staring at the pile of smoldering rubble through the windshield mottled by rain drops. The site where the building stood hours ago appeared through the rain as a blurred mess of destroyed or damaged structure and stalls, tangled pipes and vats. He expected to see remains of stables in the debris left behind by a barn fire. The rest was suspicious.

The volunteers finished fighting the fire except to ensure nothing flared up and to keep any curious onlookers from destroying the scene. Fatigue and his throbbing knee caused Barber to wonder for the hundredth time if he was getting too old for this.

Thankfully, one of the volunteer's spouses brought a thermos of steaming coffee and muffins for the drenched firemen. He set the coffee on the dash and peeled the paper off the muffin before shoving half in his mouth. It was no surprise when she showed up since the people in the community were always ready to help.

Barber sent everyone but the Clermonts home. He needed them until the Fire Commissioner arrived. He didn't expect the fire to flare up; not in this rain. But having someone with him as backup added a level of comfort. Fire Commissioner Thomas Wade must have broken the world land speed record as he arrived much sooner than expected. As Barber descended from the truck, an RCMP vehicle also turned into the lane. Barber shuddered at the thought of the beige sedan that tried to run him off the road.

He shook Commissioner Wade's hand and introduced himself to the RCMP officer, who said his name was Cook. It shocked Barber to learn the man standing in front of him was an inspector, not a rank one would expect to come from the detachment nearby. He was more likely stationed in Winnipeg... about 150 miles away. Barber surmised he was working at the closer detachment when the call came in.

The inspector wasted little time. "You reported a beige car trying to run you off the road?"

When Barber nodded, he continued. "We found a beige car matching the description on a side road a few miles out of town. It was unoccupied. We think someone picked up the driver by helicopter. There were marks where it appears to have landed. We saw the tracks and took photos before the rain obliterated them."

Barber's eyes widened. "Wait! A helicopter? Wha..?"

The inspector stopped him before he could go further. "Are you positive the car came from here?"

"I can't be sure." Barber shook his head and shrugged. "I saw the sun glint off something as I drove up the road and it appeared to come from the end of the lane."

"Have you been able to look inside the rubble?"

"No, I kept my people away in case there was another explosion and to preserve the scene."

"Okay, let's walk around the site. Watch where you walk though. We don't want to destroy the evidence."

Barber winced as he pushed off on his bad leg. Thoughts jostled for space in his head as he hobbled along with the two men. *What is going on? A helicopter? An inspector at the scene? The odor and appearance of a meth lab? This must be big.*

They sloshed through puddles as they made their way around the perimeter of the smoldering ruins. The remnants still-standing at the front had obstructed the view of the contents of the building although Barber had his suspicions from the section he could see. Even though he had experienced many things in his career, his heart rate sped up when they arrived at an area of the structure where the blast occurred. The devastation was complete, yet telltale signs remained of what had gone on in the barn. Round different-sized drums rested on their sides, twisted by the concussion. Mangled pipes connecting various vats lay warped into unusual shapes. Melted plastic chemical containers lay under smoldering wood.

"Better get dry powder on this." Commissioner Wade pointed to a flickering flame.

Barber waved to the Clermonts to bring a fire extinguisher.

The threesome stepped over and around debris as they walked. The odor of soaked and burned wood hung in the air but the sickening stench of rotten eggs and chemicals once again assailed Barber's nostrils. He nearly bumped into Inspector Cook who had stopped at a pile of rubble just inside where the wall stood a short time before. The inspector put on gloves and held his hands out to soak them in the pounding rain. He dug through the debris, tossing charred wood fragments and crumpled cans aside, his gloves smoking from still-hot embers hidden from the rain. Barber warned him fire might still erupt or an explosion occur, but Cook continued undeterred.

As the inspector moved more of the debris, Barber understood what Cook had seen. The legs of a body appeared out of the rubble. Cook uncovered the rest, burned beyond recognition. He checked the carotid artery for a pulse, but the man, if in fact it was a man, was dead.

Inspector Cook stood, coughing as he pulled his collar up to ward off some of the rain. He regarded Barber and Wade. His lips forming a straight line, he said grimly, "Gentlemen, I'll get the medical examiner here and take pictures." He walked away, his head bowed.

Barber guessed from the inspector's reaction he knew more than he let on. Maybe Cook even knew the deceased.

# CHAPTER FIVE

Inspector Cook spoke on the phone with Nathan Harris' superior, FBI Special Agent In Charge Charles Walker. Walker lived in Atlanta and, while he was Harris' boss, he was also one of his closest friends. He approved the alias for Harris using the credentials of a deceased man who had been imprisoned on drug charges in Illinois. The man had no family and his death by natural cause went unreported to the public. Walker then assigned Harris to go undercover to find the kingpins of an international crystal methamphetamine business distributing the deadly drug throughout North America.

They worked with the assumption that the Mexico border through which most of the drugs enter the U.S. had become too challenging so the organization established a production center in Canada. Harris' work unexpectedly led him to a farm near the small town of Cedar Valley, Manitoba where he discovered an industrial-sized operation. The product supplied western Canada and the northwestern United States. The FBI and RCMP launched a joint investigation when they determined the operation had international implications.

The FBI has authorization to carry out routine investigations within a 50-mile radius of the Canada-U.S. border under the Smart Border Declaration signed in 2011. However, they considered this case far from routine and the RCMP sanctioned Harris' work in Canada. The project became known as Operation Silent Running.

Now Harris might be dead. The body size and shape matched. The autopsy results would provide answers soon. Cook said to Walker, "Charles, Nathan identified the distribution network in Canada to us, but we waited to hear further from you. Is there anything new on your end?"

A king-sized lump in Walker's throat forced him to swallow twice to find his voice before answering. He was suffering from the apparent loss of a good friend. To Cook, he presented his stoic professionalism. "No, Nathan had free reign in this operation. He wanted to minimize communication with us to avoid detection so we maintained silence. If they uncovered his identity, I'm not sure how they could have done it. It might have been careless handling of the chemicals that caused the explosion, but Nathan wouldn't be negligent if he was doing it. When do you expect the results from the autopsy?"

"It will take a while, but I asked the M.E. to give me anything to confirm the identity as soon as he finds it. As you know, we have all of Nathan's information in the unfortunate circumstance we might need it."

Cook inhaled before continuing, "We're tearing apart a sedan the local volunteer fire department thought might have come from the farm where the barn blew up. Our guys found the car abandoned a few miles out of Cedar Valley. The driver tried to run the fire department off the road. It's possible the driver was trying to delay the department to give the blaze more time to destroy evidence. So far, the sedan is clean. No fingerprints. Nothing. The registration belongs to a farmer in another town about 50 miles away who reported it stolen the night before. It looks like the driver prearranged an escape by helicopter. There are marks from the helicopter skids where it landed."

Walker hesitated before speaking. "The explosion has the earmarks of a professional hit." He expounded on his theory to test it with his counterpart from the RCMP. "The organization did a lot of work using a farm as a front they would eventually just abandon, but the cash inflow from their sales would far exceed any outlay. They picked a small town in rural Canada where they thought no-one would ever find them. They might have planned to wind down at the location. Harris became expendable, so they sent in a squad to take him out. He was just a driver and worker. They could pick a new one up anywhere. He represented one too many witnesses. The hit team prearranged a pickup time for evacuation by helicopter and they will move somewhere else. What do you think?"

"It works for me. The theory holds together."

Walker continued with his theory, "From what Harris told me about the operation, it was sophisticated. My understanding is they mixed anhydrous ammonia and lithium with iodine crystals and water to create the meth. Both could be explainable since farmers use anhydrous ammonia in fertilizer and lithium to make batteries. However, the drug lab would need substantial quantities. They extracted the meth with a solvent and turned it into crystals by putting sulfuric acid through it. They also used cold remedy medication purchased or stolen in huge quantities from a pharmacy somewhere, extracted the medication from the pills and added the meth. Then they buried the whole thing in a pile of grain and shipped it by truck. He hadn't been able to locate the U.S. destination yet though."

Cook chimed in. "The vats contained miniscule traces of chemicals. They cleaned them well. The whole thing is unbelievable. They ran the business right under the noses of a small community. No-one asked questions because it looked legit on the surface. I'm sure the farming activity itself came up in conversations over coffee at the local café. What do you want us to do from our end?"

"Without Nathan we aren't any closer to the person in charge. Meanwhile, more lives are being ruined. I suggest you see if you can determine the identities of the farmers. We'll also alert every law enforcement agency to be on the lookout for pop-up farming operations here in the U.S. That's all we can do for now."

"Okay, we'll continue our work on the car and see if we can find the farmers that worked the land. We'll squeeze them if we find them. We'll alert our law enforcement about the farming scam, in case they try to start up in Canada again. Oh, wait a minute..."

Cook put his hand over the phone leaving Walker waiting on the other end. Cook's voice broke through Walker's thoughts about his friend. "Well, I have good news. The victim isn't your man. The M.E. says the silver fillings in Nathan's teeth identified in his file don't match the teeth belonging to our vic." He added, "The initial findings are that the guy died from shrapnel thrown from a metal container."

Walker's head dropped forward and his shoulders sagged in relief. His friend and colleague survived the blast or was somewhere else when it occurred.

But huge questions remained.

Where was Nathan Harris now and why hadn't he called?

# CHAPTER SIX

The blast knocked Nathan unconscious for a few minutes, but the stables and vats sheltered him from the brunt of the detonation. The shock waves tossed his body against siding that survived at the back of the barn. As he came to, searing flames licked around him and an acrid smell filled his nostrils. He needed to move, so he used every ounce of strength to crawl through a gap in the wall to a patch of grass where he collapsed.

When he awoke the second time he sensed it had only been minutes since he passed out. He willed his muscles to roll onto his back. His ears echoed with white noise, but he thought he heard distant sirens. It may have been his imagination playing tricks since he *expected* the fire department to be coming. He laid unmoving for a few minutes, assessing the damage. As his mind gathered thoughts one by one, he enumerated the effects on the human body of a blast such as the one he experienced. Many gruesome possibilities existed, but the most likely would be damage to the ears and lungs and the effects of flying debris. His ears hummed but the approaching sirens registered, signaling the return of his hearing. His lungs burned, but not from the catastrophic damage explosions can cause. He had cuts and bruises, but no broken bones so he considered himself to be very fortunate.

Nathan checked behind his back for his gun. It wasn't there. A scan of the area revealed the handle sticking out of tall grass where it must have fallen. He stumbled to pick it up and pulled himself together enough to trudge into the field behind the yard. Now he needed time to consider his options. If anyone found him alive, they would want to talk to him or worse. Had the person who caused the explosion survived? The man turned to run when the blast occurred, but it happened so fast he was likely killed.

Nathan half walked and half ran, his boots picking up wads of mud, for about a mile into the field to the safety of a clump of trees. Even with his fuzzy thinking, he surprised himself by remembering the name for a grouping of trees on the Canadian prairies - a bluff. The middle offered protection from the rain and cover if anyone came looking for him. With his back supported by a tall Manitoba maple, he tilted his head against the tree bark and fell asleep.

Rustling leaves jolted him awake. A check through the shattered crystal of his watch told him it was around 2 a.m. The noise was more than the wind or drops of water falling from the leaves. Something or someone approached through the brush. He reached behind his back and drew his gun. Only his eyes moved as he scanned the dark underbrush and the shadows of the trees.

He waited.

There! Something brushed by a branch, bending it forward and letting it go. It swooshed back into place. Whoever, or whatever was being careless.

Then he saw it.

Eyes pierced the dark a few feet away on his right. Only an animal. But Nathan kept his gun ready just in case. The coyote trotted past, oblivious to Nathan's still body, but it picked up speed, perhaps disturbed by the odor of smoke and chemicals on his clothes. He fell asleep again.

Nathan awoke with the sun's rays snaking through the branches. He had remained in his spot all night, shivering from shock and the relentless rain that continued well after he escaped from the scene. He groaned as he got to his knees and stood to move to the outskirts of the trees where the sun shoved the clouds out of the way.

Water droplets splattered on him from the branches above as the wind shook the leaves. It felt like every muscle and ligament of his body had stretched to its breaking point. Still, he considered himself lucky. As much as his body hurt, it was still intact. He assessed his injuries again and found only a few cuts and a body that ached every time he moved.

He needed to decide his next move. So far, he had only identified the minor players in the organization, but he caught a break in the last few days. Or thought he had. The organization scheduled the final load for shipment to the U.S. and they wanted him to drive. It represented the break he was waiting for, but the opportunity had blown up along with the barn.

How did the organization identify him? Or was he giving them too much credit? Maybe he became expendable because he was too familiar with their activities. Or had someone betrayed him? The only people aware of his assignment were Charles Walker, his superior at the FBI, and Inspector Cook from the RCMP. *It couldn't be them, could it?* It wouldn't be long until the newspapers announced only one person died in the blast and the organization would realize the one person was their man. His life was in jeopardy, but so many possibilities existed, he wasn't sure who his enemy was or from which direction they would come.

He considered Naomi at home in Atlanta. She knew he was on assignment somewhere. That's it. So unfair to her. He missed her. He promised himself to call as soon as he had the chance. But what would he tell her? That people he worked for manufactured and distributed crystal meth and they somehow discovered his identity? That they tried to kill him? *Oh, and her life might be in danger too?* There were too many reasons not to call her.

So many questions. Nathan sat down, his head throbbing. He needed to make a plan and, for now, to stay dead.

# CHAPTER SEVEN

Naomi Bedford finished her long day of work at a trendy woman's wear shop in downtown Atlanta's Peachtree Mall. Two days ago, she used her discount at the store to buy a crew neck black-and-white striped top and knee-length skirt, which she wore today.

She rocked back and forth in unison with the other passengers as the train rolled towards her condo in the suburbs. The words on the pages of her book blurred as her attention drifted elsewhere. Nathan Harris hijacked her thoughts. He often occupied her mind since he went away, but more in the last few days.

Nathan left town on assignment weeks ago and she'd heard nothing. He kept the details of his mission to himself, tossing out the old line that "the less she knew the better." She gave him a hard time even though she knew leaving bothered him. Now things had changed.

They met about a year earlier while standing in line for coffee at Starbucks. He caught her eye when he walked in the door right after her. Tall and good looking in a rugged David Beckham way, she judged him to be in his early forties. The dark wavy hair and 5 o'clock shadow contributed to his sexy demeanor. The tan leather bomber jacket over jeans and a black merino wool ribbed sweater he wore to offset the unexpected cool weather in Atlanta didn't hurt either. He stood in line behind her and commented on the chilly day. The initial small talk led to sharing stories on warm places they'd visited and they chose seats at the same table to enjoy their drinks and continue the conversation.

Naomi considered herself to be plain, but she captured male attention with her blond hair and slim figure. It must have worked on Nathan as he called to ask her out a few days later. One date led to several more. Easy conversation and good sex followed and her friends congratulated her and told her how cool it was she dated an FBI agent. He even carried a gun. But since Nathan's disappearance off the face of the earth, she questioned their relationship.

There was no doubt she liked him a lot. Maybe love would even blossom with time. But living with questions bothered her, not knowing where he was or what he was doing or if he was even alive. Military spouses handle their husband's absences all the time, but it didn't mean she had to or even could. What if she fell in love with him, got married and one day a knock came at the door announcing a thug had killed Nathan while he was on duty? She didn't want to be in continual fear of losing him.

The conclusion for Naomi was that she wasn't capable of doing it. She needed to tell Nathan when he returned. But then something else happened making her even more sure.

She ran into a man in her condo building who attracted her attention. It started innocently enough at the beginning as it had with Nathan. He introduced himself as Simon, and he asked if she had a boyfriend. She told him she did, but he worked for the FBI and his assignment took him out of town. Noticing her despondency, he invited her in for coffee. He focused his attention on her as she poured out her feelings about Nathan and his job.

As the relationship developed, she saw him often and enjoyed his company. She soon ended up in bed with him. The attraction was instantaneous, as it had with Nathan, but more visceral. She knew she should stop, but she couldn't.

Now guilt enveloped her as the train drew near her stop. Her actions with Simon weren't a mistake because she liked her new lover. But she wondered if Nathan missed her. Was he thinking about her and looking forward to seeing her?

Naomi hated that idea. She chastised herself for her weaknesses. It wasn't the first time she cheated on boyfriends. Why couldn't she keep a relationship? She should have never allowed herself to fall for Simon, not when Nathan was away. He deserved better. He was just doing his job. She had to explain everything as soon as she heard from him.

She got off the train at her stop, changed into jeans and a tee shirt and climbed the stairs to Simon's condo where she tapped on the door.

# CHAPTER EIGHT

Nathan decided he had to walk back to the yard to find something, anything, that might help him locate the home of the American operation. And what of the grain truck? They wouldn't leave a truckload of product sitting in the yard, would they? It made no sense. He wanted to check it out.

It was dawn, so it was doubtful anyone was in the yard unless the RCMP left an officer to guard the crime scene. He'd handle any eventuality when he arrived at the site.

The walk to the yard through the soggy field was slow and painful, but the warm sun beaming from the cloudless sky on this fall day loosened his sore muscles. It felt good to stretch, and he lengthened his stride as he walked. As he got closer, the stench of wet, burned wood and chemicals filled the air.

He crept forward behind the cover of trees to discover the yard abandoned. Yellow police tape fluttered in the wind around the perimeter of the barn, and markers designated where the debris fell. He knew the RCMP would do a thorough job of taking photos at the crime scene and documenting what they discovered.

The grain truck still stood beside the bin. Minutes passed as Nathan walked around the truck undoing the ropes holding a tarp covering the truck's grain box. One corner was already loose, but after undoing the rest, he pulled the heavy canvas covering to the back and grabbed a shovel propped against the granary. With a grunt, he stepped onto one of the dual tires at the rear of the vehicle, tossed the shovel into the box and pulled himself over the edge after it.

Standing knee deep in wheat, he probed the grain with the shovel. He was looking for a duffel bag containing around 45 pounds of packaged crystal meth with a street value of close to a million dollars. The space he uncovered at the front of the load exposed nothing. He moved wheat around in the middle. Still nothing. He slogged through the grain to the back and shoveled it to the middle of the box. They hadn't buried the product in the grain despite what they told him.

This suggested three things. The first was that the RCMP found it. He doubted that as the tarp hadn't been disturbed except for the loosened corner. The second was that plans changed and they moved the product another way. The final one was more sinister. They never intended him to drive to the U.S. but used the explanation as a ruse to get him to the farm.

Questions remained: where did they go and how did they transport the last shipment? Nathan had confirmed that product remained for delivery the day before the explosion. They must have moved it during the night. Meth weighing 45 pounds didn't require a lot of space. There were many ways to transport it.

He climbed gingerly out of the truck box and tried the door handle of the cab. He smiled when he depressed the button and the door opened. The keys dangled from the ignition, the interior of the cab reeked of cigarette smoke and fast food wrappers littered the passenger seat. The ashtray overflowed with cigarette butts. He ran his hand under the seat, looking for anything unusual. Nothing. When he opened the glove compartment, he discovered that someone, probably the RCMP, had removed everything. They would have confiscated the registration. He slammed the door as he jumped to the ground. He shivered as the pain that raced through his body when he landed reminded him that it would take time to fully recover.

A quick glance at the highway going past the farm assured him no one was going by to see him walking to the pile of debris where the barn once stood. Ducking under the tape, he walked into the area. The police could arrive any minute to continue their investigation so time was at a premium. At least the still-standing front portion of the barn offered protection from being seen from the road.

He picked his way around and through the burned stables and the twisted metal and plastic that were integral pieces of the industrial laboratory. He didn't know what to expect, but he hoped for something that would give him a clue where he should go next. The search could be futile. If everything else failed, he might take a chance and call Charles Walker to find out if he had more information. Should he go back to Atlanta? He needed assurance he wasn't missing something. He still didn't know if someone at the highest level exposed his identity. Who could he trust?

Nathan worked from the front to the back, kicking pieces of metal and plastic and tossing others aside as he went. Clouds of ash floated into the air, clogging his airway and making him cough. The RCMP had removed everything they considered important, including his phone that had been sitting on the barrel. He assumed the phone would not have survived the blast. But there might be something else left that would be helpful to his investigation. The still-standing ragged siding at the back where he landed during the blast came into view. He regarded the gap in the boards where he escaped. After three passes of the barn, working the space like a grid, his experienced eye noticed everything, but nothing that would help him.

After several minutes of futility, the time came to abandon the search and walk to town to find a phone. Walker had to be trustworthy. They had known each other for years. His best bet was to walk through the fields to avoid any possibility of being seen. He ducked under the tape and headed to the page wire fence used in Canada to keep livestock in place. It separated the farm from the neighboring property. He turned to scan the yard before climbing the fence. There was nothing to see, so he put his foot onto a strand of wire midway up the fence to hoist himself over.

A piece of paper stuck in the barrier about fifteen feet away caught his eye. Someone had crumpled the paper into a ball as if they wrote something and discarded it.

This could be something. Or nothing. He climbed back down from the fence and ran to grab the paper before it became dislodged and floated off in the wind. He smoothed it out on his knee, his eyes widening as the paper unfolded. It was a handwritten commercial invoice displaying a quantity of goods along with a value. The invoice was for a load of grain, but someone had written a dollar value, scribbled over it and entered a new sum.

As he examined it, he surmised the person preparing the document intended it to be part of the paperwork required by Customs to export goods from Canada into the United States. Instead of using documentation on which the writer changed the product's value, they filled out a new form to avoid suspicion and for easier entry into the U.S.

To Nathan, the product description and value meant nothing. What mattered was the buyer's address. It was the information he needed.

He had a new clue and it lay in Fargo, North Dakota.

# CHAPTER NINE

Nathan's progress across the stubble field was as fast as his sore limbs allowed. He alternated by walking and resting, always staying out of sight of the road. As he neared town, he ensured he was far enough away from the farmer repairing something on his combine in the field to be unidentifiable.

He needed to get to Brandon to continue the journey to Fargo. He couldn't walk into the Now's The Time café and ask for a ride. That would arouse suspicion for sure. No, he needed to borrow a car. He wanted to find one the owner wasn't likely to miss for a while so he could drive to his destination before anyone reported the theft. The best place to find one was at the café. A few minutes waiting in the shadows beside the gas station across the street paid off when an elderly farmer parked his pickup truck and made his way inside the restaurant.

The old boy would sit in the café with his friends long enough to gossip, most likely about the explosion, and enjoy a cup of coffee and the obligatory piece of cherry pie. Nathan hustled to the truck and tried the door. Just as he suspected, the farmer left it unlocked. People trusted each other in Cedar Valley. They would question their trust when they learned the truth about the Decker place and what he planned to do next.

The pickup was an older model, which made hot wiring possible. He climbed in on the driver's side, a breath of relief escaping his lips when he reached under the steering column and pried off the plastic cover. Fortunately, plastic clips held it in place so there was no need for a screwdriver. He pulled bundles of wires free from the wiring harness connector.

By following the wires with his fingers, he discarded the bundle leading to the left of the column for the lights and turning signals and to the right, which provided power to the wiper control. Based on the colors of the wires left in his hand, he twisted the ignition and battery wires together so the car would continue running when he started it. Country music suddenly blared from the radio, so he spun the dial until he heard a click to silence it. In the final step, he sparked the starter wire against the battery wire and the car was his. Two minutes had expired when he pulled away from the café.

The drive to Brandon was without incident. He stopped for a few minutes on a side road to throw the gun he had been carrying into a pond surrounded by weeds and bulrushes. Taking it across the border would raise too many questions and besides, he could pick one up without a problem in the U.S. The marsh swallowed the weapon, so he doubted anyone would stumble across it for years.

He stopped at the motel where he paid the final balance on his room, changed and grabbed his belongings and the extra cash he had hidden. The next stop was at a retail store to buy a prepaid cell phone and a SIM card for use in the States. Since there were no flights from Brandon to Fargo he parked the truck on a side street a few blocks from the bus terminal. After purchasing his ticket as David Penner with cash and climbing into the bus, he settled into his seat for the two and a half-hour trip to Winnipeg. He considered the ever present closed circuit security cameras prevalent in public places. They were something he had to be aware of at all times.

As the bus pulled out of the terminal, he called the local police department anonymously to report the location of the abandoned truck. He thought of contacting his boss in Atlanta, but he still questioned whether someone in the FBI office had connections to the meth organization. The same questions applied to the RCMP. The situation required a low profile for a while longer. He would take things as they came and keep a watchful eye for any danger. Golden crops waving in the wind on the flat prairies all the way to the horizon sped by. The crops soon faded to black as the empty seat beside him allowed the opportunity to stretch out and drift into a fitful sleep for the rest of the ride.

The rustle of his fellow passengers moving in the now still bus awakened him. It startled him to see the sign designating the Winnipeg terminal staring back at him through the window. He must have been sound asleep for the trip's duration. Stiffness greeted him when he moved, but his mind felt more alert. His body required rest and the bus ride provided the opportunity.

The bulk of the money belt under his shirt pressed into his flesh as he got up from his seat. He had depleted it, but a count at the motel confirmed enough to buy an airplane ticket to Fargo, rent a room and car and buy a gun. A little remained for food. He didn't want to leave a credit card trail of his travels.

A taxi took him to the airport and as he pushed through the revolving door, he surveyed the terminal for security cameras. He walked with his chin pointed to his chest and his baseball hat pulled low to avoid detection. He worried the next challenge could come when he tried to clear U.S. Immigration and Customs before boarding. If the FBI or RCMP had issued a bulletin for his whereabouts, he could be in trouble.

The departures board confirmed a flight would leave soon. While he waited after securing a ticket, he used a public computer terminal to research the drug scene in Fargo. It ranked fifth among U.S. states with the lowest incidences of drug problems. He realized the minimal drug scene made Fargo a good place from which to distribute illicit drugs. Less suspicion.

Ticket in hand, he shuffled along the pre-clearance line. The bored-looking Immigration officer waggled his fingers at Nathan to step forward. He gave Nathan's documentation a cursory look and glanced up to confirm his photo. Nathan answered the standard questions, and exhaled a sigh of relief when the officer said, "Have a safe flight, Mr. Penner." The official showed no sign of concern nor was there any suggestion of an outstanding bulletin.

He strode up the ramp to the plane and received a broad smile from the attendant for showing his boarding pass. A small bottle of wine purchased from the same attendant during the flight settled the adrenalin rush, allowing him to rest. Thanks to timely connections and after a 4-hour flight and a stop in Minneapolis, he arrived in Fargo at 10:30 pm.

He tossed his belongings into the back of a rental vehicle and stopped at a motel to register. Most travelers freshen up after a plane trip, but he did just the contrary. He tousled his hair and grabbed the clothing he wore the night of the explosion from his suitcase. The smell of smoke, chemicals and body odor floated into the room. He hadn't shaved since he left home. It was difficult to stand himself but the reflection in the mirror told him he looked the part.

It was time to go after the head of the snake.

# CHAPTER TEN

With the help of the GPS in the rental car, Nathan drove through the dark to the address on the invoice he found on the Decker property. Away from the city lights, the nickel-silver moon shimmered through the thin cloud layer and the stars took turns poking through when they had the chance. He turned the heat on in the car to ward off the autumn chill.

He wished he had a weapon, but that had to wait until the stores opened in the morning. As he drove, he wondered if the street number was legitimate. The organization wouldn't want to raise suspicion with an address someone could figure out to be fake. If it was real, it may have no connection to the drug business.

It didn't take long to find the location west of Fargo. A sign at the entrance announced the street number and the name North Country Grain Growers. As Nathan suspected, it appeared from the outside to be a legitimate facility. It looked as advertised, a place to buy grain having nothing to do with the drug part of the business. A drive around the parking lot confirmed in his gut it was a complete waste of time. It was time to move on to the second and more dangerous part of his plan.

Despite the lack of drug culture in Fargo, there would be users somewhere. Experience from other busts gave him confidence he could find them. It didn't take long driving the streets until he found the seedier neighborhood every community has but wish they didn't. He parked three blocks from the neighborhood and walked towards it.

After finding the street that interested him, he staggered as if under the influence. A streetwalker sauntered in his direction wearing a tight sweater, short skirt and stiletto heels. He took in her features before going into his act.

There were none of the telltale physical signs he was looking for, but he took the risk and asked with slurred words, "Know where I can get hot ice?" He expected her to recognize one of the street names for the drug.

She fired back, "You a cop?"

He staggered backwards as if to fall and she leaned forward to grab his shirt.

He mumbled, "Thanks, not a cop. I'm hot railing, but I'm coming down. I need a score fast."

"Okay, I don't do that stuff, but I'm aware from other girls there's a house on 44th Street. You could try there. You driving? If you are, you shouldn't be."

He weaved on his feet, mumbling, "I'm taking the bus." He gambled it hadn't stopped running for the night. She would think he was stoned, anyway. He continued, lifting his head. "Where on 44th?"

She gave him directions to get off at the cross streets near the house. "Your stop is three blocks from the house. Hustle. The last bus leaves in ten minutes." Then she added, "Now get lost. You're scaring away the customers."

Nathan turned and staggered back toward his car. Her raised voice echoed through the night air as she pointed in the opposite direction. "You're going the wrong way, dumbass. The bus stop is the other way." He shuffled his feet in the opposite direction and nodded to her as he tottered past, feigning the shakes. After half a block, he noticed a police car driving in his direction along the street. Nathan glanced to see the hooker had disappeared, so he straightened his shoulders and walked so as not to attract attention. The officer checked him over and continued driving.

He circled the block to avoid being seen by the streetwalker. The bus roared by, its air brakes squealing as it pulled up to the stop. It was of no consequence. When he arrived at his car, he started it and drove towards 44th Street. The streetwalker waved when he passed by but he looked away. A quick check in the rear-view mirror told him she must have assumed another potential customer had ignored her and continued on her way.

At 44th, he cruised along the street until he found a house fitting the general description she had given him. It was a decent enough neighborhood, and he was sure it would shock the neighbors to know what was happening in their midst. He parked the car a few blocks from the house and walked up the steps to the front door. A few lights shone past the pulled blinds. He rang the doorbell and waited.

No response.

He tried the door handle, which turned with no resistance. As ordinary as the house appeared on the outside, inside was different. Mattresses lay strewn on the floor of the living room. The occupants had scattered syringes and pipes beside the makeshift beds. One person lay passed out on the mattress. Nathan resumed his act, staggering past the room to the bathroom where users often smoke their drugs to take advantage of the fan's ventilation, but it was empty.

Sounds caught his ear from the second floor so he pulled himself up the stairs maintaining his performance for anyone who might be watching. *How in God's name didn't the neighbors notice people coming and going?* He shook his head and continued to climb.

A male and female occupied a room next to the staircase. They lay clothed on the bed, glassy eyed and, Nathan guessed, beyond capable of conversation. They wore filthy clothes, the man unshaven, and both looked and smelled as if they hadn't washed in weeks. He asked from the doorway, slurring his words, "Do either of you know where I can get crystal meth?" He pronounced it "crishtal mef." The woman stirred and groaned while the man stayed unmoving. He tried again. "Any chance I can get meth?" No response.

This was hopeless. He planned to return before he called the local authorities to report the place. He turned to leave, walking along the hall towards the stairs before a weak female voice called after him from the bedroom. "Wait."

The woman poked her head around the door frame holding a frail finger to her lips and pointing with a shaking hand at the main floor. She followed Nathan downstairs and signaled for him to go outside through the front door. He stopped on the porch with the woman falling in behind him.

A longtime user stood before him. Her sunken cheeks were close to translucent and her hair was receding. Her eyes protruded and two front teeth were missing. He tried to guess her age. If he didn't know she was an addict, he would guess she was in her seventies. He suspected she was in her forties.

She gazed at her shoes, but she murmured, "Why are you looking for meth?"

He responded with his own question. "Why does anyone?"

She raised her chin, scanning his face with her bloodshot eyes and her next response chilled him. "Can you help me?"

"What do you need?"

"Help me get off this. I'm sick. I will die if I keep going as I am. If you help me, I can help you. You aren't a user. I can tell. You're lookin' for a dealer?"

There was no reason to maintain the facade. Even in her addled state, the woman had seen through him. He wasn't sure she could help him with what he was looking for, but he was determined not to leave her here if she wanted help. "I can get you help. I'll call an agency and someone will come and get you out of here. You'd better go when they ask you to leave. The police will shut this house down in the next few days. Understand?"

"Yes. Please do as you promise." She turned her hunched shoulders to drag herself back into the house.

Nathan spoke to the thinning hair at the back of her head, "What's your name?"

He watched and waited. She turned back towards him, still examining her torn running shoes, her voice a whisper. "My name is Mandy... Mandy Montgomery." Every word took everything she had. She faded, her head lolling to the side.

Nathan put one hand on each of her bony shoulders and shook her.

"Mandy, look at me. Look in my eyes."

She tried to do as he asked, but her eyes darted everywhere. Her lips barely moved. "I overheard the dealer talkin' bullshit to a guy downstairs yesterday. He talked 'bout where they make the stuff. He was a big loud guy." She inhaled with a ragged breath before continuing. "He talked big, kinda showin' off, as if he was the boss or somethin'. The guy saw me at the top of the stairs. He pointed at me and shrieked if I talk to anybody, he'd come back and kill me." Her round shoulders shuddered. "I'll tell you one thing. He was a scary son of a bitch. I believed him."

The woman wobbled on her feet and her eyes rolled back in her head.

Nathan exhaled. He realized he'd been holding his breath. "What else did he say?" He leaned with his ear to Mandy's mouth to hear her next words.

"He said they make the stuff at a dairy farm two miles south of town."

# CHAPTER ELEVEN

Mandy hadn't given him much and offered nothing more. She fumbled with the door handle until Nathan helped her inside the house. With his arm around her waist, he guided her upstairs to the bedroom and left her on the bed.

His burner phone was only good for phone calls so he got into his car and drove until he found an all night Internet café. Inside, he rented a few minutes of Internet time, chose a machine and looked up the phone number for an addiction recovery center and the address for a gun store. Back outside in the car, he called the addiction center hotline and left an anonymous message telling them about Mandy, along with the street address for the house. He hoped she would allow herself to get the help she needed and seemed to want. The police wouldn't be far behind closing the house. If the other inhabitants didn't want help, they would find another place to crash or become part of the street scene.

He followed I-75 south of the city with the odometer ticking off the miles. Would he find the right property in the dark even if he stumbled across one with potential? Even the moon wasn't co-operating now as it hid behind a dense cloud cover.

The organization's standard operating procedure of hiding in plain sight, at least using Manitoba as a model, meant the myriad of side roads and farms provided many places to disguise a drug lab. The options narrowed if Mandy's estimate of the two-mile distance proved to be right, but did she mean two miles from downtown? Two miles from the city limits? He would drive around until he found it.

The tires hummed on the pavement pulling him away from the city. The shadow of farm buildings loomed ahead, a silo towering over the others. It was worth a try. They wouldn't run their operation within a few hundred yards of the main highway, would they? A quick check of the odometer told him he had traveled two-and-a-half miles from the city limits. He turned onto a side road and cruised past the farm. Vehicles and machinery stood in the yard's darkness. No sign of movement. A light illuminated a large barn, but the house remained dark. Not surprising considering the time. Four legged shapes stood unmoving beside the barn. He identified them as black and white dairy cattle huddled together in the pen. The familiar butterflies, the sixth sense telling him he was close to something, fluttered in his stomach. *This might be it.* He needed to get closer.

Nathan left the car on a lane off a side road a mile further east of the farm. He forgot the stiffness in his body as adrenalin pumped through his veins. His route through a field took him past an uncaring herd of cattle. His dark moving shape disquieted a few horses sharing the pasture. They shifted and snorted their concern.

He crouched behind a tractor hitched to a machine on his approach from the dark side of the barn. Sensing no one around, he continued, catching himself before stumbling over a mound of discarded bottles and containers. There was no sign anyone heard him when he stopped. He picked up and sniffed a bottle and a strong chemical odor aggravated his nostrils. Every pound of methamphetamine produces six pounds of toxic waste so it would not be surprising to see the containers strewn on the property... if it was the right place. The shapes, sizes and odor of the bottles hinted at a meth lab. The signs were adding up in his favor.

Crouched beside a barrel and hidden by the shadow of the building, he poked his head around the corner. Light gleamed from inside through the uncovered windows. The fact the windows had no cover bothered him. Maybe this farm *is* legitimate, he thought. Then a strong chemical scent like rotten eggs drifted towards him. It didn't originate from the pile of bottles. The rollercoaster of thoughts experienced in the last few minutes veered again towards believing he had found the right place. If he was right, the barn's size suggested an even bigger lab than the one he found in Manitoba.

He needed to find out more and somehow identify the person or people in charge. There could be dozens of facilities like this scattered across North America. Nathan had to look through the window. He took one step around the corner and froze. A tiny light flickered in the darkness at the front of the building that wasn't there a minute ago. He recognized it. Someone had stepped around the corner and lit a cigarette. Nathan drew back into his hiding spot.

A trickle of sweat slithered down his spine. Too close for comfort. He peered around the corner, watching from the cover of his hiding spot until the man returned inside. He wore farm clothes so he might be doing chores. If there was a lab, they would separate it from the farming operation similar to Manitoba. Perhaps it would be better to see it in daylight instead of stumbling around in the dark. He decided he would stake out the farm in the morning.

The horses nickered their anxiety again as he retraced his steps across the field. His stomach growled as he drove back to the motel, reminding him he hadn't eaten all day, except for a small bag of pretzels provided by the airline. He pulled into a fast-food joint and ordered a pepperoni pizza. It was not the best choice given the hour, but he would improve his eating habits when he was home. Back in the motel room, he showered, ate half the pizza and stored the rest in the mini fridge.

As he leaned against the headboard with his arms folded behind his head, he pondered his situation. Had he ever felt more alone? He thought of Naomi, but each day away convinced him more she couldn't support the crazy career he had chosen. It was too unpredictable, and he had learned Naomi was someone who required stability. It would be unfair to continue the relationship. He didn't blame her. In fact, he respected her for it.

His mind drifted back to the case. He should call in

reinforcements but the nagging question resurfaced. *Who had tried to have him killed?* Someone from the local police force might even be on the organization's payroll. He would call Walker once he had more information. *Walker couldn't be dirty, could he? And what about Cook from the RCMP?*

A forbidding shroud of loneliness draped over him.

He often used a trick to fall asleep when something weighed on his thoughts. He refocused to draw attention away from what was bothering him.

As he closed his eyes, he remembered he needed to buy a gun. At least that was something he could control.

# CHAPTER TWELVE

Nathan awoke to the sun dodging the blind by sneaking through the gap between the window covering and the wall. With one eye closed, he squinted at the clock radio beside the bed, which read 8:10 a.m. He paid little attention to his surroundings when checking in, but now sitting up and looking around confirmed it was another nondescript motel room: one chair on which he threw his clothes the night before, a flat screen TV on a cheap dresser, a mini fridge, a desk with a lamp and an office chair. He recognized Bourbon Street in New Orleans in the framed print on the wall. At least the bed was firm although it enticed its occupant towards an indentation in the middle. It was preferable to the tree he slept against the night of the blast.

He turned on the TV and thumbed the remote to flick through the channels. There was nothing describing the explosion at the farm in Manitoba, but he suspected the Canadian news stopped at the border. Or the story had used up its share of the news cycle. A plane rattled the windows of his room on its final approach to the airport forcing him to turn up the volume. The shrieking jet engines hadn't jar him awake during the night so the wind direction must have allowed the pilots to use a different runway.

After getting dressed, he enjoyed a cup of coffee and bacon and eggs at the small restaurant attached to the motel. By the time he finished, the store he Googled the night before would be open. He confirmed he didn't need a license or registration to buy a gun, but he needed his FBI credentials for a concealed weapon permit. Within minutes he owned his favorite weapon, a Glock 19, a holster for the small of his back and a box of ammo.

He purchased a screwdriver from a hardware store next to the gun shop, returned to the motel and unscrewed the back of the television set where he hid his FBI credentials. After reattaching the back of the TV, he loaded the Glock and lifting his untucked shirt, seated the weapon in the holster on his back and headed out the door.

On the way to the farm, he stopped to pick up enough snacks and water at a convenience store to hold him over during a stakeout. He realized sitting in the car would draw unwanted attention so he planned to settle into a bush across the road. The cloudless sky reflected a brilliant azure color, but the sun was taking its time heating the day. The only sweatshirt his size was a navy blue beauty sporting "Fargo Rocks" in bright yellow lettering across the front. Not great camouflage. It was preferable just to tough out the cold.

He parked the car in the same spot as the night before, stuffed his supplies in his pockets, checked his gun and crossed the same field. The cows showed mild interest, and the horses continued grazing, paying no attention this time. He settled behind a bush from which the farmyard was visible, prepared for the tediousness of a stakeout.

There was little activity throughout much of the morning. A couple dressed in coveralls and work boots left the house and ambled to the barn. Although a worn cap shaded the man's face, Nathan thought he was the one who lit the cigarette a few hours earlier. The farmers worked inside for an hour before leaving in their car. A younger man, perhaps a son in his teens left the house later in the morning, went into the barn and remained there. The kid was a younger version of the man. His bouncy stride mimicked his elder, and he dressed the same.

A half ton truck drove into the yard around 11:30 a.m. and two hulking men descended. Nathan perked up, on high alert. He knew one. He met him at the farm in Manitoba. His name was Larson and from conversations Nathan had had with him, he owned a record for drug-related offenses. He bragged about crimes involving violence, and from what Larson said, they were escalating in severity. The man knew his way around the lab in Manitoba.

The two men sauntered towards an equipment storage shed at the back of the property. *Maybe the barn wasn't the lab after all!* Nathan estimated the steel building to be over 200 feet long and almost as wide. The only windows were near the top of the rounded peak. An overhead door, wide enough for heavy equipment, dominated the front of the building while a smaller door for easier people's access stood to the side. The men stopped at the smaller door. Without binoculars it was difficult to tell, but judging by the time they stood at the door before entering, Nathan suspected there was a combination lock keeping it latched.

He had to learn what was happening in that shed. But how? It looked impenetrable. Now he noticed the security cameras on the building's eaves making matters even worse. He hadn't seen them the previous night in the dark. It didn't appear to be a sophisticated system, but it complicated matters further. Maybe the farmer installed them to deter would-be thieves. *What was the role of the farmers? Were they simply supplementing their income?*

Once again, he weighed calling the local authorities but it would only force the organization to move to another location where they would restart their business within weeks. No, this had to stop. He had to do more. From his hiding spot he followed a path identical to the one the night before that brought him to the location behind the barn.

Nathan peered around the corner, examining the angle of the security cameras. By circling the barn and hugging the shed's side, it would limit his exposure to the camera to a few seconds. Now, more than ever, he needed his luck to hold. It was one thing to survive the blast in Manitoba. Now the risks were high and numerous. He hoped no-one was monitoring the security system. The kid could leave the barn at an inopportune time. Someone else may be watching from the house. The men might finish their work and leave the shed. The farmers could drive into the yard. Still...

Nathan took his weapon out of the holster, took a deep breath and raced across the yard until he sidled up to the side of the shed closest to the smaller door. With his back pressed against the wall, he inched forward with the gun pointed skyward until he arrived near the front. He couldn't see anything. He couldn't hear anything. But when he passed the back, he smelled something - the familiar odor wafting through the ventilation system.

The men inside were cooking meth.

# CHAPTER THIRTEEN

The shiny steel walls stood about fourteen feet high and the windows near the top were impossible to reach without an extension ladder. Nathan thought of taking the men at gunpoint when they exited, but the whereabouts of the farmers still presented a problem. Besides, there might be more than Larson and his buddy inside.

He examined the camera at the back of the building. It angled towards a row of bushes and a field. *If the cameras aren't monitored, how long until someone checks the video feed? Or would anyone ever check if they suspected nothing?*

He leaned back with his head against the wall. He wondered how he could ever penetrate the large building without being seen. Then remembering the strong scent coming from the back, he thought about the ventilation. If the farmer built the shed for farm equipment, it required only ridge vents on the roof and along the eaves. That wouldn't be enough to ventilate the odor. He shuffled back along the side towards the rear of the building.

When he reached the back, he looked around the corner and examined the ventilation system. The noxious fumes came from a makeshift duct made of galvanized pipe forced through a hole drilled in the wall about eight feet off the ground. He placed his gun back in its holster and edged towards the pipe, never leaving the wall. From beneath, he realized the pipe wasn't large enough for his body to squeeze through. Even if he somehow pulled the pipe out of the hole after the occupants left, he still wouldn't be able to fit.

After a few seconds of staring at the pipe, he noticed someone had sealed the gap between it and the wall with a makeshift, and far from professional, combination of caulking and duct tape. He realized with some luck he might remove pieces of the tape and caulking to get a glimpse of what was happening inside the building.

Nathan needed something to stand on to execute his plan. He recalled a barrel behind the barn, but dragging it carried too much risk. He scanned a pile of junk in the bushes behind the shed. Among the detritus lay containers of various sizes, but another barrel appeared to be lying on its side. He had to risk the camera's prying lens again, but, if it was a barrel, he thought he could roll it over in a few minutes, limiting his exposure.

He hurried to the pile and confirmed a wooden barrel sat half buried in the dirt, but it had rested there long enough that a piece of the side had rotted. The top was missing. He tugged on the barrel, but it didn't budge. With both hands, he wrestled it from the ground. It was in rough shape. More wood was rotten than he liked. The barrel might not support his weight, but the metal supports holding it together seemed to be solid.

He picked up a sharp piece of silver metal from the pile and slid it in his back pocket before half dragging, half rolling the barrel to a spot under the pipe. Nathan stood it upright and tested it by placing one foot on the edge at the top and pulling his body weight up along the side of the shed. He leaned against the building so the barrel wouldn't absorb his full weight and tested the other foot. The barrel held.

Upwind from the nauseating fumes drifting from the pipe, he attacked the caulking and silver tape using the metal he found at the scrap heap. As unprofessional as the work was, whoever had taped around the pipe had taken their time and sealed it well. The caulking not so much. Precious minutes raced by as he picked and scraped until a piece loosened. The need for quiet hampered his speed although he thought the roaring fan inside the building would obscure any sound he made.

The small chunk of caulking broke loose and fell inside the building. Nathan froze. A few minutes passed without incident so he continued chipping at the caulking and pulling at the tape. He grabbed a loosened piece of tape between his thumb and forefinger and ripped it, along with a piece of caulking stuck to it, away from the pipe. The row of trees behind him offered shade, but he didn't want light flooding into the building through the hole he was creating. He needn't have worried yet. There were layers of tape. He worked at the next strip, picking, scraping and lifting. It lifted easier than the first and he continued until he removed enough of the layers to create a hole wide enough to get a visual inside.

By lifting the tape and sliding his hand underneath to cover the hole, he prevented light from entering. With his hands blocking the light on either side of his face, he leaned in towards the hole. Although the gap wasn't large, it afforded him a view of the scene in the building. Shock raced through his nervous system. The Manitoba operation paled by comparison to this. They had created a room segregated from the front of the shed and what he saw was a super lab. It was large scale with pressurized containers connected by wires and coiled tubing, plastic barrels, mixing trays and a stack of finished product Nathan estimated to be worth millions of dollars. The weapons stacked in the corner were even more disturbing.

One man busied himself stuffing the product inside children's toys. Nathan surmised they shipped the toys to low level dealers across the country who extracted and distributed the product.

Another sudden chill slithered down his spine. *Why only one man? Where was the other one?*

He sensed rather than heard the sound behind him. He turned to see Larson standing with one hand supporting an armful of garbage and the other holding a semi-automatic pointed at him.

Nathan Harris knew his luck had run out. _

# CHAPTER FOURTEEN

*Penner*!? Is that you?

As Nathan turned, Larson's body stiffened. "Why are you here, man? You're supposed to be dead!" He threw his armful of junk towards the pile. "You should have died in that explosion in Manitoba." Despite his surprise, the gun barrel never wavered.

Larson's shock escalated to anger forcing his lips to purse together. He gritted his teeth. "And why are you spying on us? Hoping for a piece of the action? You have much explaining to do, my friend." He gestured to the row of bushes. "I noticed you're carrying. Throw the gun and that metal tool in your hand away and get off the barrel."

Larson wiped saliva from his mouth with his free hand. His eyes were bloodshot and glassy. It was obvious he had been sampling the product which made him unpredictable. Nathan removed the Glock by the handle from its holster with his thumb and forefinger and tossed it and the metal piece he had been using to scrape the caulking towards the trees. He jumped from the barrel with his hands in the air and grimaced with the landing. Sweat trickled along a path between his shoulder blades and his palms were damp. Staying calm was a priority right now. The only good news so far was that Larson referred to him by his alias so at least they hadn't uncovered Nathan's identity, or if they had, Larson was unaware.

He tried an explanation. "C'mon Larson, put the gun away. I found out you were in Fargo from some users. I heard of your action here from guys on the street. I thought they were full of shit, but I wanted to see for myself. Turns out they were right. So were you. Yes, I want part of the action, but I wanted to see it before talking to you. You guys went inside and I was glad you were there man because you'd listen to me. I planned to follow you when you came out and get you by yourself so we could talk."

The corner of Larson's mouth tilted up, his eyes narrowing. He wasn't buying it, but his drugged state made him talkative. "Lucky for you the boss is coming to inspect the operation. He wants confirmation on how much we're producing here. Make sure we're not stealing, you know?" His lips curled in a sneer. "You can tell *him* your little story. See if he believes it. Let's go."

He grabbed Nathan by the shoulder to stop him and checked his pockets before shoving him toward the corner of the building. As the two walked around the corner towards the front of the shed, he waited for Larson to let down his guard. The opportunity didn't come. Larson stayed far enough back so even if Nathan made a sudden move to disarm him, he might get off a shot. Nathan wondered if the man would shoot if he made a run for it. There was no reason he wouldn't and even in his drugged state, with a semi-automatic weapon he could fire enough shots in Nathan's direction it was likely one or more would hit him.

He had to let this play out and bide time for the right opportunity. Hours and hours of training told Nathan to wait even though his situation was serious.

They arrived at the front door and Larson motioned for him to stand off to the side while he punched in the combination. The door opened, and he motioned with his weapon for Nathan to step inside the building. Lines of fluorescent lights illuminated the shed. Farm equipment lay scattered on the concrete floor throughout the expansive space.

They walked past the implements to an unlocked door leading to a well-appointed workshop. Metal cabinets lined the walls and tools covered the bench. More tools hung in neat rows from brackets on the walls. Larson pushed Nathan towards a sheet of metal leaning against the wall on the right side of the bench. With the gun in his left hand still pointed at Nathan, Larson heaved the metal sheet aside, exposing another door.

As he shoved Nathan through this door into the drug lab, he announced, "Hey Sebastien, we have company."

The other man, wearing a mask and coveralls, concentrated on stirring a concoction in a barrel. He turned down a blaring radio, stopped stirring and glanced up at Nathan. "Who's he?" he asked, pulling the mask from his face.

"Remember the guy we tried to kill in that explosion

in Manitoba? Penner? This is him. He was at the back looking through a hole by the vent pipe at us."

Sebastien Garcia threw the mask on a mixing table and left the stick in the concoction, but picked up a rifle propped against the bench. He sauntered over to the pair until his face was inches from Nathan's, his long dark curly hair hanging over his rugged, bearded face. His dark eyes bore into Nathan's for seconds until he spoke with a thick Spanish accent. "And why were you looking at us?"

Nathan tried his story again but this time the response was the butt end of the rifle jammed into his solar plexus. His air left him with a whoosh and as he leaned forward the rifle butt slammed against his head. He crumpled in a heap on the ground, gasping for air. He opened his eyes at the last second to see a worn leather work boot streaking toward his face. Turning his head deflected the blow, the boot just missing the mark. The movement saved his teeth but his jaw took the full impact and a burst of brilliant flashes erupted in his head.

Through the haze, he heard Sebastien tell his colleague to tie him up and put him on a chair. Nathan still gasping, squinted through his swelling eye at Larson who left through the door and came back moments later with zip ties. He yanked Nathan's arms behind his back and slipped a tie over his hands, tightening it on his wrists to the point of strangling his circulation. Nathan tried to fill his lungs when Sebastien hauled him to his feet and forced him onto a wooden chair. The air was slow in coming. A shock wave traversed from his cheek through his body, forcing a groan.

His head lolled to the side as he felt his feet tied together with the plastic restraints.

Garcia yanked Nathan's head up by the hair. His face was so close that Nathan sensed a hint of garlic on his breath. A trickle of blood slithered down Nathan's swollen chin. Ignoring the pain from his cheekbone and the areas where the rifle butt hit him was difficult since he wasn't sure which hurt more. Garcia sneered, "I don't know what your real name is and I don't care why you are here. The only thing keeping us from torturing you and burying the pieces in the field is that our boss is coming for a visit this afternoon. He will want to interrogate you himself before he kills you."

Nathan stared into Sebastien's dark deadly eyes, saying nothing.

He was in a lot of trouble.

# CHAPTER FIFTEEN

Garcia and Larson were having a heated, but muted discussion behind stacked containers in the farthest corner of the room. Nathan strained to listen to the raised voices and caught enough of the conversation to recognize Garcia's anger with Larson for dipping into the product. Larson replied he hadn't taken enough for anyone to notice, but Garcia didn't want him anywhere near the person they kept referring to as the "boss." It sounded as if Garcia forced his words through clenched teeth. "He will tell by your glazed eyes. Make yourself scarce when he gets here. If he even thinks you have been sampling the meth, he will kill you. I've seen how he gets with my own eyes. Now, clean the containers and straighten this mess. He'll be here soon."

Larson dialed the radio back up to drown out the fan noise and did as Garcia told him. Nathan sensed Garcia approaching so he hung his head as if semi-conscious. Garcia stopped in front of him and slapped him on the face. "Listen Penner, or whatever your name is. You haven't got long to live, my friend. Your story better be a good one. Think of something and he might let you live a few minutes longer."

Nathan noted neither man was familiar with his identity. He took a chance at incurring Garcia's wrath again. He spoke through clenched teeth, but loud enough for Garcia to understand. "You're aware they tried to kill me in Manitoba, right? They missed. I got away."

Garcia shrugged. "It was me who drove the man to the farm to blow up the barn. He never returned, so I thought he was killed in the explosion. That mistake made the boss very unhappy."

"Why did the boss want me dead?"

"Ah, you became expendable my friend, a witness to our little enterprise. We planned to destroy the lab since it had been in one place long enough. The boss likes to move around. We never intended to bring that last shipment here. We wanted to lure you to the barn. The idiot we picked to do the job panicked and blew up the building and himself but didn't destroy the equipment and didn't kill you." The point was made emphatically in Spanish. "Idiota! No loss he's gone. And you, you are still expendable. You will be next."

Nathan drew in a breath with the answer. No one in the FBI or RCMP betrayed him, but it was too late. He should have called Walker to tell him what he was doing. He could have called Naomi. Not trusting his friends might cost him his life.

Nathan locked eyes with his captor. "Aren't you concerned you will become expendable too? If this so-called boss wrote me off, aren't you afraid the same thing will happen to you? That would worry me if I were you."

The other man choked on a laugh. It came out as a grunt. "Not likely, my friend. I have the advantage." He turned to walk away, but tossed back over his shoulder, "The boss is my brother."

Nathan's stomach flipped as if the bottom had dropped out of an elevator. Convincing Garcia to worry about his own situation might have worked, but he hadn't counted on them being siblings. Garcia turned his attention to cleaning the lab. Nathan strained at the zip ties restraining his hands. They cut into his wrists, cinching them tightly together and numbing his hands. He looked for any sharp object nearby he might use to cut through or at least weaken the plastic. There was nothing within reach.

Wriggling his fingers helped work out the numbness. He needed more feeling to find the ratchet mechanism locking the tie. His ligaments and tendons strained in his hands as he stretched until he found the mechanism on the side of his left wrist. Not the best place for his plan. It might be possible to snap the tie if he maneuvered the ratchet to a spot between his wrists and applied enough downward and outward pressure. His captors remained at the other side of the room so he caught the ratchet mechanism between his wrist and the side of the wooden chair and manipulated the restraint. After several tries, the tie moved an inch. He tried again and again until he thought the ratchet mechanism was where he needed it.

The next step was riskier. He searched for Garcia and Larson again and was grateful to see their cleanup occupied them. The radio blared alternative rock music. The fan roared to clean the air. His stomach lurched and stars flashed in his eyes as he stood. His head and face throbbed, suggesting a concussion and maybe a broken jaw. He had to persevere. As he stood, he raised his arms behind his back as high as they would stretch. He dropped them hard towards his backside while applying outward pressure on the plastic ties. The ties held. He tried again.

Nothing.

The beating had weakened him. The maneuver worked many times at the Academy, but he had been healthy then. It was successful nine times out of ten. He sat and rested for a few seconds, glancing at Garcia and Larson. He had to keep trying. His life was at stake. Ready to try again, he checked over his shoulder once more to satisfy himself Larson and Garcia were still busy.

He tried three more times, but the ties held in place. He plunked himself in the chair, defeated. Nathan took several deep breaths. He had to wait awhile until he tried again. He hoped each attempt weakened the ties and the next try would work.

A noise through the walls captured his attention. It was difficult to hear above the noise in the room, but the same sound preceded the blast in Manitoba. It was a muffled car door slamming.

It was too late.

He was about to meet the boss.

# CHAPTER SIXTEEN

Nathan watched as a tall man with a brown complexion strolled through the door. He wore a navy blue suit, starched white shirt with a plain burgundy tie and matching pocket square. It was classic business attire, but the man wore it well. It looked tailor made and expensive. He glanced at Nathan before wandering over to Larson and Garcia. After acknowledging the man, Larson kept his head bowed and hurried through the door as his partner suggested he do.

The "boss" and his brother hugged and whispered. Nathan strained to hear their low voices. Their glances drifted in his direction, and he surmised they were talking about him. The man strode towards Nathan after the conversation ended.

He stood in front of Nathan for a full minute before speaking. Then, "You are a difficult man to kill Mr. Penner. I doubt that is your real name since you came this far to find us, but you made our job easy. I sent men to find you after I found out you didn't die as I expected you to, but you were on your way here. Why did you come to visit us?"

Nathan remained stoic. "You first. Who are you?"

"Ah, you're putting up a brave front, I see, and foolish too. Well, never mind. My name is Garcia. Camilo Garcia. I am his brother." He gestured towards his sibling who busied himself tidying up the room. He gestured around the room with his arm and expounded as if he felt the need to explain. "This is not what I do for a living, but it supplements my income so I can buy expensive toys and retire soon in my country."

Nathan wondered what he *did* for a living, but it didn't matter. There were many questions. Had the drug lord's brother been telling the truth when he said they wanted to get rid of him because he was expendable? No matter what happened, Nathan wanted to learn the truth.

"Why did you try to kill me in Manitoba?"

"My brother Sebastien said he told you it was time to move the operation. The plan was to make it look like an accident and pin the blame on you for cooking the meth. The man my brother used screwed up by blowing himself into a million pieces and he didn't even destroy the equipment. It makes me angry when I think about it. When we finish here, the poor farmers will suffer a similar fate, but there will be no mistakes this time." He raised his voice to stress the last part of the sentence as his brother stood with his head bowed.

He continued, "But enough. There is no time for conversation. You need to say your final prayers."

The hair stood on Nathan's arms and at the back of his neck, but he refused to show fear, except he might be a shade paler now than he was from the beating. He concentrated on his pain to focus his thoughts. "Look Garcia, I'm with the FBI. I've alerted my colleagues concerning your lab. They know I'm here and if I don't call in by 5 P.M., I've requested that they move in on you. It will go much easier for you if you let me go."

Garcia regarded him, tossing his head back in a hearty laugh. "Good one, Penner. My brother vetted you in Manitoba. Even searched your room. He may choose terrible friends but he is thorough at checking people. You're not FBI. I believe you when you told my brother you want a piece of the action. You seem to be a bright guy. But the time we take to walk to the field will decide how long you live." He yelled to his brother, "Sebastien, get Larson and let's go. I want to see this guy dead so I don't have to think about him anymore."

Nathan was startled by what Camilo said. The boss would be furious when he found out Sebastien screwed up twice. Once by choosing the wrong person to blow up the barn and a second time when he told his brother Nathan was not with the FBI. Sebastien wouldn't have found anything, anyway. But the fact he confirmed to his brother that Nathan was not FBI, when in fact he was, would not sit well with Camilo. Nathan tried to figure out how to convince Camilo he worked for the agency to pit one brother against the other. He filed it away for the moment.

Sebastien replied that he would call Larson when they got outside the building. He used a box cutter to slice the plastic restraint around Nathan's ankles before grabbing Nathan under the arms and hoisting him to his feet. Nathan's cheek brushed against the man's shoulder and pain penetrated his head once again.

Nathan staggered on his numb feet as Sebastien pushed him towards the door. The trio marched through the shed with the boss bringing up the rear. Nathan saw Sebastien grab a rifle before leaving the room, but Camilo appeared to be unarmed. When they reached the door leading to the outside, Nathan squinted until his eyes grew accustomed to the brilliant sunlight.

"Larson, come here!" Sebastien's raised voice traveled across the yard, but no response was forthcoming. He tried again, but the other man didn't respond.

Nathan tried again, "I suspect my FBI colleagues caught him."

Camilo was not amused. "Shut up with your FBI talk." He said to his brother, "I'm aware Larson's been sampling the product. If he's smart, he left and will keep running. He will be the next one buried in the field."

As they turned the corner toward the trees, Nathan searched for a way out. He would die fighting if he had to. The distance between his back and the end of Sebastien's rifle was about two feet. If he turned quick enough and used his body to knock the gun aside, he could maybe stun Sebastien with a head butt so he could run. But there was still the matter of Camilo, plus the fact his head was still woozy and his hands useless, tied as they were. The circulation in his feet had returned, but did he have the strength to do anything?

They neared the field. He had to do it now. He counted on Sebastien being focused on the thought of killing him.

Nathan drew in his breath to eliminate the cobwebs from his head. He centered himself, concentrating on his next move.

His muscles coiled like a cobra ready to strike.

He was ready.

Now!

At the instant he was set to launch himself, the crack of a high-powered rifle shattered the quiet. The sound waves echoed across the field and rebounded from the tree line. A second shot erupted from the same spot.

Nathan ducked to make himself a smaller target. He heard the second bullet whine off the dirt behind him and thud into the side of the shed. His mind erupted in a jumbled mass of thoughts. *What the hell just happened?* He turned to see Sebastien lying crumpled in the dirt, his eyes staring at nothing and a hole in the side of his head oozing blood. Camilo ran crouched past Nathan towards the front. A third shot kicked up dirt at Camilo's heels.

*Who the hell is shooting?* Even with limited possibilities, Nathan didn't have time to think about it, but he knew it wasn't the FBI. Everything he told Camilo was bullshit... just a bluff. The FBI didn't even know he was in North Dakota. As he had done in the shed, he raised his arms as high as possible and snapped them down and outward trying to break the plastic tie. It didn't work. The pain blinded him for a few seconds. He staggered toward the front of the shed.

*The plastic must be weakening by now.* He slowed to a stop and tried the maneuver one last time. He summoned everything he had, his muscles straining. It broke! His hands were free. Thank God! He had to go after Camilo. He rushed back and forced the rifle from Sebastien's fingers. Camilo disappeared, but if Nathan hustled to the front, he might get a shot at him.

He ran to the front of the shed and turned the corner to a shower of dust and gravel from Camilo's spinning tires battering the metal siding as he sped away.

# CHAPTER SEVENTEEN

Nathan raised Sebastien's rifle to his shoulder, but the car swam in and out of focus as he tried to sight along the barrel. He worried if he took a shot, it could go wide and into a neighboring house. Dejected, he lowered the rifle and watched the car race along the lane towards the highway. The sound of running feet somewhere near the tree line caught Nathan's attention for a moment, but another sound distracted him. Someone had fired up the tractor he hid behind last night.

The tractor emerged and moved parallel to the car on a trail used to haul manure to the field. A manure spreader jounced along behind. The trail the tractor traveled turned to run parallel to the highway, but the driver steered straight into the steep weed-covered ditch towards the pavement. He was running in high gear and Nathan gasped when two wheels on one side of the tractor lifted as it swerved off the well-worn path into the ditch. The spreader rocked back and forth shifting the tractor's center of gravity. Whoever was driving didn't slow as the tires churned and the machine wavered on the brink of overturning.

Yellow and purple flower petals burst into the air as the machinery plowed through the weeds. The motor groaned and belched a puff of smoke as the tractor re-established its equilibrium and thumped down on all four wheels. It jerked and rocked again as the front wheels found the upward slope of the ditch towards the pavement.

Garcia reached the highway, the car's tires squealing in protest and depositing a trail of black rubber as it fishtailed onto the asphalt. Nathan sensed the running footsteps drawing closer, but his eyes remained glued to the bizarre scene unfolding in front of him. It was as if he was watching a movie. Garcia floored the accelerator and the car's powerful engine howled its response.

The tractor continued its relentless climb, but its forward momentum slowed as the front of the spreader dug into the dirt on the upward slope of the ditch. The engine persevered, dragging the front of the spreader through the dirt until it joined the tractor on the slope. As the machine's front wheels hit the shoulder of the highway, the cab's door flew open and someone climbed onto the hitch leading to the spreader.

The person stood perched on the hitch for endless seconds, his arms flailing as if he was surfing a wave in Hawaii. Finally, he took a death-defying leap to the side, away from the fast-moving machinery. His momentum sent him rolling and twisting into the ditch as the forward wheels of the spreader roared past within inches. The tractor and spreader continued unabated onto the highway and towards the opposite side.

While struggling to straighten the fishtailing car in his haste to get away, Garcia must not have seen the tractor until the last second. Tires squealed sending puffs of blue smoke into the air when he applied the brakes. The car swerved to miss the enormous machine, but it was too late. The impact of the 4,000 pound car colliding with the much heavier tractor shook the ground. Engines howled and metal screeched as the two vehicles melded together. It was like two rhinos charging and meeting head on in a death match. The speeding car's forward momentum pushed the tractor sideways until the thick tread on the rubber tires grabbed the pavement. Time slowed as the tractor teetered. The car continued until the tractor overturned with a breathtaking thud.

Everything ground to a halt. Only the tractor's topside rear wheel turned until the big engine choked out its last dying breath. An eerie silence hung suspended in the dust above the carnage as smoke poured from the car's crushed engine compartment and liquid dripped from both vehicles. Nathan had been transfixed, but he shuddered, peering through the haze for a sign of life. Nothing moved.

The running footsteps closed in and would turn the corner any second. *Larson!* It had to be. So much had happened he'd forgotten there was a third man. He whirled with Sebastien's rifle at his hip, ready to fire as Larson rounded the corner.

But it wasn't Larson.

The farmer Nathan saw leaving with his wife in the morning stopped and bent with one hand placed on his knee. The other hand held a Remington deer rifle with a scope. He gasped, digging deep for breath. Nathan realized now his foggy brain had not registered the farmer's car back in the yard. The farmer wheezed, "C'mon, that's... that's my son on the tractor. You cover the son of a bitch in the car." He took off with his free hand holding his side. As Nathan ran after him, countless questions tumbled over each other in his head. *What's going on here? Was Larson in the car with Garcia?* The rifle hung from the farmer's hand as he ran. Did *he* shoot Sebastien?

The dazed son dragged himself out of the ditch as his father and Nathan arrived. Nathan judged him to be about fifteen years old. His hat was missing, revealing a mass of unruly blond hair. A lump was taking shape under scarlet road rash on his pimpled cheek and he limped towards his dad. The farmer threw his arm around his son's shoulders and Nathan heard him ask, "James, you okay?" Despite everything he had been through, the young man nodded his head and grinned.

Nathan reached the wreckage and aimed the rifle at Garcia, who hung forward on the collapsed air bag, which draped over the steering wheel like a sheet. The man wasn't moving. Nathan looked in the back seat. No sign of Larson. He reached in and pressed his fingers against Camilo's carotid artery. He stepped back with the rifle still pointed at Garcia and looked over the tangled metal at the farmer and his son. It was impossible to tell where the car ended and the tractor began. The spreader became unhitched during the collision and deep ruts in the pavement led to where it lay on its side a few yards from the wreckage.

He yelled, "Do you have a mobile phone?" When the son answered in the affirmative, Nathan said, "Call 911. Tell them to send everybody."

# CHAPTER EIGHTEEN

More surprises were in store for Nathan Harris. The farmer confirmed his son was okay and then signaled towards the barn. The door swiveled open, and a man emerged with the farmer's wife behind him. She held a Remington deer rifle the same as the one her husband carried, and she aimed it at the back of the man walking in front of her. Plastic zip ties bound the man's hands behind his back. It was Larson and when they drew closer, Nathan noted four ties secured his hands. He would not be escaping.

Police and emergency vehicles arrived a few minutes later. In the meantime, Nathan called Walker in Atlanta to check in and so his boss could confirm his identity to the police. His FBI credentials would have to stay in their hiding place in the television until later. Walker fired questions at Nathan, but he had no answers yet. From Walker's tone, he would get an earful for not trusting his superior and friend when he got back.

The paramedics loaded the unconscious, but still breathing, Garcia into the back of the ambulance and examined Nathan.

His jaw was bruised, and he had a concussion. The paramedics expressed their concern, but they went along with Nathan when he promised to check himself into the hospital after he talked to the family.

With Nathan's agreement, the local police interviewed each of the people involved individually so he didn't hear the full story. When they finished, he advised them the FBI would take the case since it had international implications and the officer concurred. His opportunity to speak to the family arose after the emergency personnel left.

The farmers took him to the house where the aroma of fresh bread met them at the door. Nathan drew laughter when he commented they should make perfume from that smell. They sat around a square table with chrome legs that could have been a hand-me-down from a parent. The source of the aroma, a bread maker, chugged away on the crowded counter.

The farmer introduced himself as James Doyle. His face was deeply tanned, and he'd earned countless furrows on his countenance from the tribulations of farming. When he tossed his hat in the corner, he exposed a full head of white hair. His wife's name was Mary, and their son, James Junior. Handshakes all around followed the introductions and Mary offered a cup of tea and a piece of pie. Nathan hadn't realized how hungry he was. A second piece followed the first as he settled in to listen to James Senior's story.

"I needed a loan from the bank two months ago. I asked for

a sizable sum to buy more cattle and the bank manager, Camilo Garcia, said he'd approve the loan if we did something for him. He surprised me since we have good collateral and always repay on time. Anyway, he said he wanted to set up a manufacturing business in the back of our shed. The business didn't need much room, he said, and since the shed is big and we don't use it much, I agreed. It was the biggest mistake of my life.

"I didn't realize they would make drugs until they punched a hole in the wall. That pissed me off. I visited Garcia at the bank to find out what they planned to do and he threatened us. He said he would kill us if we told anyone. One night he and his brother, Sebastien, came out and roughed us up. They blackened Mary's eye and burned my leg with a welding torch. See?" He lifted his pant leg revealing an ugly scar.

"We agreed, but we knew it was wrong. We didn't know who to turn to, but then I saw you skulking around. I was having a smoke in front of the barn and saw you hiding in the shadows. I was tempted to talk to you, but I wasn't sure whose side you were on. We decided we would watch you if you came back."

Nathan listened, perplexed. "Was it the security cameras?"

Doyle laughed. "The security cameras? Nah! Those damn things haven't worked since a lightning storm killed them a while back. Young James here said he would fix them, but he hasn't got around to it yet. Too busy doin' chores and checkin' out a new girl at school. Doyle laughed. "I suspect he'll impress her now with his tractor story."

Mary's brow furrowed at her husband's comment. Nathan thought he should work on his "skulking" skills, but he smiled as he glanced at the younger James. The red shade of embarrassment climbed his features from the collar up like the liquid in a thermometer on a warm day. Even the purple road rash on his cheek turned a brighter shade.

Doyle continued, "We farmers know our surroundings. Farming somehow sharpens our observation skills. That's how I saw you. Anyway, damned if you didn't turn up again today. We watched all morning for you and James was in the barn when he glanced out the window and there you were by the shed. I made sure he had the rifle in case you tried something funny. When he told us, I figured with all this sneaking around you must work for the law. At least it was obvious you weren't on the side of the Garcias so we took a chance on you. It became clearer when the banker's brother took you inside at gunpoint and then the banker showed up. We waited until Larson came out. I clobbered him with the rifle butt and we dragged him into the barn where we tied him up and Mary kept her gun on him.

"James and I took up a spot in the trees and they soon marched you towards the field. It looked for sure like they planned to kill you, so I shot the banker's brother. I had training as a sniper in my younger years so I had no problem with the shot."

Nathan raised his hand. "Wait, you've had sniper training? No offense, but you missed Camilo."

"Yeah, the guy didn't have a gun. I couldn't kill a guy in cold blood, could I? I tried to wing him. He moved fast, and I have to admit I missed. I'm out of practice and my hands are shakier than they were years ago. When I missed, and he looked to be heading for the car, I sent James to get the tractor to block him. I assumed he would head to town. If he turned the opposite direction, it could have ended a different way." James Senior reached to tousle Junior's hair. "I guess he blocked him all right. Looks like we'll need another loan for new machinery."

"Well, you all did great. If it wasn't for you, I'd be dead. I can't thank you enough."

"Ah, it was nothin'. How serious is this damn crystal meth they were cooking?"

"It's easy to make and therefore available at a lower cost than other drugs, like heroin. Seizures of meth are going up while others are declining. It often contains deadly toxins and at the least, it can have lasting effects on a person's physical health and appearance. It's also addictive. There's a pleasurable high followed soon by a devastating crash so users are always looking for their next hit."

Doyle grimaced and shuddered. "Okay, we've heard enough. I'm happy we stopped them."

Nathan said, "I have one more question. Do you think the Garcias acted alone or did they work for someone else?"

"Well, Garcia bragged about how he built his business by himself and he was a millionaire and everything. His dad belonged to some cartel in Columbia and taught him the tricks of the trade.

Nice, eh? Garcia told me one day these farming fronts worked well for him. He said he had others. He mentioned one up in Canada but the time came to move on so he ordered his crew to destroy it and kill a guy who was expendable. I don't know. I guess he was just reminding me what they could do to us. Just trying to scare us is all."

# CHAPTER NINETEEN

Nathan clutched a fresh loaf of bread wrapped in plastic while James Junior drove him to his car on a four wheeler. He thanked the young man again and promised to stay in touch with the family. He thought to himself he would try to pry compensation for the tractor out of the federal government. They could do that much for the family's part in stopping a multi-million dollar drug business.

It was a short drive well within the speed limit to the hospital where the checkup was as short as the wait was long. He thought it was a waste of everyone's time but the paramedics insisted and he had promised. When they called him in, the doctor confirmed his concussion and gave him medication intended to hasten his recovery. She suggested over-the-counter medication to dampen the pain from his check and other assorted spots on his body resulting from the explosion. The doctor examined his vision, concentration and reflexes and declared him fit to drive. When he told the doctor he planned to fly, she told him to get lots of rest before the flight, sleep on the plane and use earplugs to drown out the noise.

He drove back to his motel, retrieved his FBI credentials from the back of the television set and checked out. He struggled to make himself heard to the cashier over the screaming engines of a descending jet on its final approach to the runway. His head throbbed at the noise, confirming his next move would be the right one. He planned to reward himself with a night at a five-star hotel.

After checking in, the delightful pulsating stream in the luxurious shower warmed his body for several minutes before he put on fresh pajama bottoms. He wrapped himself in a velour bathrobe with the hotel's logo embroidered on the left breast. A call to room service promised a juicy steak, medium rare with the trimmings. His saliva glands kicked into high gear at the thought of the homemade bread Mary had given him. A few slices would be part of his dinner. When the meal arrived, a quick check of the mini fridge revealed a decent supply of beer and he downed two with his food. While his favorite was unavailable, it was not the time to be a beer snob.

He piled the empty dishes on the trolley and pushed it through the door into the hall. As relaxed as he had been for a while, he stopped delaying the inevitable. He picked up the phone, lay back on the bed and dialed Naomi.

Her cheery voice answered and for a fleeting moment, Nathan's heart skipped a beat. She chattered about how happy she was that he called and he told her what had happened while trying not to alarm her. Then, her voice becoming somber, she said, "Nathan, I have to tell you something. I can't do this. At the beginning, when you left, I was sick with worry. I couldn't sleep. I couldn't eat. It was too much. I can't deal with not knowing where you are, whether you're dead or alive or ever coming back. A person has to be so strong and I realize now I'm not."

Several emotions washed over Nathan as he listened. She wasn't the person to support him in his career. It saddened him when she confirmed his suspicions, but it relieved him on one level that Naomi recognized the same thing. He was sorry in some ways he had the career he did. Would he ever find someone?

He blurted out, "Would it help if I found a career outside law enforcement? Maybe get a legal degree so I can stay in one place?"

Naomi hesitated, but then she said, "You're so sweet, Nathan, but that work isn't enough to satisfy you. Your calling is to stop the bad guys not try to defend or prosecute them when someone else catches them. Besides, I have something else to tell you. I met someone while you were away. His name's Simon. I'm so sorry, Nathan."

New emotions broadsided him. Shock and a tremor of anger flooded through his veins. He took time to compose himself before responding. "I'm thrilled you found someone, Naomi. I hope it works out for you." Then he added, "Friends?"

"Friends for life. It was nice talking to you Nathan, and I'm glad you're okay. Take care."

And with that Naomi left his life. Nathan leaned back on the pillow with the phone resting on his chest processing their discussion. *Naomi just needed the right man.*

There's no point in feeling sorry for myself, he thought. His next call was to his superior in Atlanta, Charles Walker. Nathan brought Walker up to speed on his conversation with the farming family. Walker replied, "You've done enough on this case, Nathan. I'll send another agent up to interrogate Garcia. From what the local authorities are saying, he has lawyered up, but he wants a plea deal. He'll name everyone who worked for him, including the Manitoba crew, in exchange for a lesser sentence. He says there's another farm doing the same thing. When Larson finds out, I'm guessing he'll talk too. That's one network we can close. Great job, Nathan."

"The farmers should get the credit. They stood up to Garcia, and they saved my life. I got lucky in Manitoba."

"Oh yeah, about that. You can trust people you work with, you know."

"Sorry Charles. I had too many questions when they tried to kill me. I was sure they discovered my identity. Everything pointed to someone telling them I worked for the FBI."

"Okay, okay, I get that. Now, get your rest. Take the time you need. I have a new case I want you to take on when you're ready."

Nathan's mouth curved into a tight smile. His friend was making sure he got back on the proverbial horse.

"Really? What is it?"

"It's a human trafficking ring involving African girls and the Tanzanian police are looking for help. Are you interested in a trip to Dar es Salaam, Tanzania in a few days?"

Exhaustion overtook Nathan as the weight of the last few days descended on him. "Sounds like just what the doctor ordered," he mumbled as he ended the call, let the phone drop and fell into a deep sleep.

<<<<>>>>

*Never So Alone* is a prequel to Book 2 of the *Marcie Kane Thriller Collection*, *A Perilous Question*. Thank you for reading. If you liked what you read, please consider taking a moment to leave a review at your favorite online book store.

# ABOUT THE AUTHOR

Barry Finlay was raised on a farm in Rapid City, Manitoba, Canada before becoming an accountant. He is the award-winning author of the inspirational travel adventure, *Kilimanjaro and Beyond – A Life-Changing Journey* (with his son Chris), Amazon bestselling travel memoir, *I Guess We Missed The Boat* and three Amazon bestselling and award-winning thrillers, *The Vanishing Wife, A Perilous Question* and *Remote Access*. Barry was featured in the 2012-13 Authors Show's edition of "50 Great Writers You Should Be Reading." He is a recipient of the Queen Elizabeth Diamond Jubilee medal for his fundraising efforts to help kids in Tanzania, Africa. Barry lives with his wife Evelyn in Ottawa, Canada.

Author Website: www.barry-finlay.com

Facebook Page: https://www.facebook.com/AuthorBarryFinlay

Twitter: https://twitter.com/Karver2

Fundraising website: www.keeponclimbing.com

# THE MARCIE KANE THRILLER COLLECTION

## (AVAILABLE INDIVIDUALLY OR AS AN E-BOOK BOXED SET)

## BOOK ONE

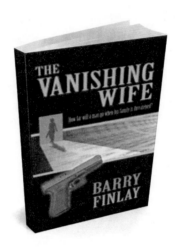

The Vanishing Wife: An Action-Packed Crime Thriller (Marcie Kane Book 1) - Mild-mannered accountant Mason Seaforth is forced to exchange his computer for a Glock 17 after his beloved wife Sami disappears the night of their 20th wedding anniversary. He and his friend, Marcie Kane, uncover his wife's staggering past that takes them on a deadly search from their hometown of Gulfport, Florida to Ottawa, Canada.

Turn the page for a preview of the first book in the *Marcie Kane Thriller Collection.*

# THE VANISHING WIFE

by

Barry Finlay

DAY 1

# Chapter 1

Mason Seaforth was waiting.

It was 6 o'clock in the morning, and the darkness in the suburbs had begun to ease. The sun would soon make its appearance for another day, causing the shadows to beat a hasty retreat. Mason was now restlessly sitting on the couch in the sunroom that belonged to him and his wife Samantha, or Sami as she was known to her friends. He was staring at the walls and thinking that if he smoked, now would be a good time to light one up.

He hated waiting. Mason was a very punctual man and had always had the attitude that everyone's time is precious. He never wanted to give the impression that his time was more valuable than anyone else's. His wife was no different. She had always had the same attitude as he did, and together they'd earned the reputation of being the "Early Seaforths." That's what made this so unusual and frightening at the same time.

Mason was waiting for Sami.

It had started out to be an amazing 24 hours. They had spent the day relaxing, exploring the area around St. Petersburg, Florida and enjoying each other's company. It was that delightfully peaceful time of year on the beach between the departure of the snowbirds back to the north and the invasion of the tourists from Europe. They had wandered around John's Pass at Madeira Beach, leisurely strolling in and out of the various shops lining the walkways. They had held hands as they walked along the beach, feeling the sun drenching their skin.

As they did so, the wind rustled through the palm fronds, sending shivers through the tall grass that separates the beach from the traffic noise on the street. They'd looked into each other's eyes as they enjoyed crab-stuffed mushrooms washed down with Coronas at Sculley's, their favorite hangout.

It was their 20th wedding anniversary and Mason had never been happier. At 48, he was in the prime of his life. He was a mild-mannered accountant who had worked his way into the position of owning his own firm. He worked hard at his one-person operation, but that suited him just fine as it gave him the flexibility to come and go as he pleased. Since meeting Sami 22 years ago, she had become his entire world. She worked as a financial advisor in the bank where Mason kept his investments, but it wasn't until Mason decided he needed additional advice on his current fixed-interest rate instruments that their paths actually crossed. The attraction was instant and intense. As he walked through the door of her office, he couldn't help but notice how attractive Sami was. And when she spoke, Mason's heart skipped a beat. Her dark auburn hair was drawn back off her face, emphasizing her beautiful features. Her green eyes were large and seemed to draw him in as he advanced towards the chair. Her lips were full, a feature he had always found attractive. When she stood to greet him, he noticed her business attire of a pale yellow blouse and dark skirt on her shapely 5'5" frame. Business attire to anyone else, but to Mason it was beyond sexy.

Sami's confidence and professionalism, along with her beauty, won him over in a way no other woman ever had, and after making up excuses to go back and see her a few more times for financial advice, he worked up enough courage to invite her out. After a short courtship, they were married, and life for Mason had been wonderful with every passing year. At 46, Sami was two years younger than her husband, and still very attractive. Mason was only too aware of the admiring glances that inevitably came her way as they walked down the street.

But he felt confident that she was more attracted to him than she could ever be to anyone else. Their anniversary had been perfect. They had agreed to celebrate the entire day together, and the hours had flown by as they drank too much wine and ate too much steak and lobster over a candlelight dinner at home. They'd laughed as they donned bibs and sprayed juice from the cooked lobster everywhere while cracking the hard shells.

Reminiscences came easily, and they shared memories that would only be funny to them. As she loved to do, Sami teased Mason about how he'd run into the wall in the dark in their hotel room while they were on their honeymoon. She unsuccessfully tried to stifle the wine-soaked gales of laughter as she recalled the black eye that Mason sported for the rest of the trip.

When dinner was finished and the last of the wine consumed, they brought their anniversary to a close by heading into the bedroom early and making love passionately. As Mason reflected on that part of the evening, he recalled that their clothes had come off urgently on the way to the bed with an intensity that was unusual even for them. He also recalled that Sami seemed even more passionate than usual. When they were finished, she had tears in her eyes and her voice quavered slightly when she told him she loved him. But she'd assured him it was only because her feelings were so strong and she was only thinking about how happy she was.

Afterwards, they had both fallen into the deep sleep that only lovemaking brings. Around 4 a.m., Mason had awoken. He felt that something had awakened him. He felt confused and groggy, but he forced himself out of bed and staggered to the bathroom. He was sure his stupor was not only from sleep but strongly enhanced by the effects of the large quantities of wine they had consumed just hours earlier. He could still smell the lingering scent of Sami's perfume.

As he stood naked in front of the mirror washing his hands, he smiled at the thought of the last 24 hours, and his tired reflection smiled back. Mason shut off the bathroom light before opening the door so as not to awaken the slumbering Sami. As he felt his way around the bottom of the bed in the blackness, he thought that she must be curled up on the far side because he only felt empty space where her feet should have been. As he climbed into bed, he suddenly sensed an eerie emptiness in the room that shouldn't have been. He reached across the bed to fold Sami into his arms. She wasn't there.

With a jolt, Mason got up again, battling the stupor that he was still feeling, and threw on the blue robe Sami had given him last Christmas. He unplugged his cell phone from the charger in the bedroom and glanced at it as he always did when he first got up. There had been no calls. He went downstairs to the living room. No Sami. Their daughter Jennifer had left for college earlier in the year, and they both missed her dearly so he went back upstairs to check her room. Maybe Sami was missing Jennifer a little more because of their anniversary and had decided to spend the last part of the night in Jennifer's bed. But she wasn't there, either. Mason padded down the hall to the room they had converted to an office, but again there was no sign of Sami. He called out nervously into the silence. "Sami? Sweetheart, where are you?" There was no response.

He decided to check their favorite room, a combination sunroom/entertainment area. They often spent their mornings there sipping coffee, or evenings together with Sami curled up beside him on the couch to watch something that they mutually agreed upon after much playful negotiation. They had splurged a while ago on a 60-inch TV and determined that the sunroom would be the place for it. Now, Mason wondered if maybe Sami couldn't sleep after all the wine and was watching TV quietly with the headphones on. He made his way into the room to check, hoping against hope to find her there. His heart sank when there was no glimpse of Sami.

A creeping uneasiness began mounting against Mason's will. He went to the back door, turned on the outside light, and stared out into the darkness of the back yard through the window. His hand shook slightly as he unlocked the door, hesitated, then called out for Sami into the night. There was no answer. Mason went back inside and opened the door leading from the front hall to the garage to see if she might have gone there for some reason. He switched on the light as his bare feet felt the coldness of the two steps to the grey concrete floor of the garage. He walked around his Audi, checking inside the vehicle as he went. There was barely room to walk between the tools hanging on the wall and the sides of his car, but he squeezed by to open the garage door to the driveway to ensure that her Miata sports car was still there. It stared back, mocking him.

After closing the garage door again, Mason returned back inside. He stood frozen, uncertain and increasingly tense. What was going on? Where was Sami? Where was his wife? Mason couldn't think. He still felt strange and detached, almost as if he was in a dangerous dream that wasn't real. Why couldn't he wake up?

And now it was 6 a.m. The sun would be coming up momentarily. There was no Sami and no question of going back to bed, so Mason finally went to the sunroom couch where he sat despondently, waiting and flipping distractedly through magazines. But he couldn't focus on the words in front of his eyes.

The anniversary clock they had been given by his parents sat on the mantle ticking loudly, interrupting the silence that permeated the room. Each tick was a reminder that his wife was gone and he was alone. Then a moment of hope sprang forward: what if Sami hadn't been able to get back to sleep and had decided to go for a walk in their quiet residential neighborhood? It was, after all, a very safe community. She was in all likelihood just out for some fresh air to clear her head, especially if she'd felt as groggy as he did.

Sami never went anywhere without her cell phone, and if she had gone out for a walk, she would certainly have taken the phone with her. He reached for his own phone and dialed Sami's number. The number rang. And rang, and rang again. Mason held his breath. "Please, Sami, please, pick up," he whispered. On the sixth ring, he heard Sami's confident voice message. "You have reached Samantha Seaforth. Please leave a message, and I will call you back."

In a shaking voice, Mason heard himself doing as she asked. "Sweetie, it's Mason, I'm leaving a message. Where are you? Please call me back right away."

It had been two hours since he first noticed Sami was gone.

## THE MARCIE KANE THRILLER COLLECTION

## (AVAILABLE INDIVIDUALLY OR AS AN E-BOOK BOXED SET)

### BOOK TWO

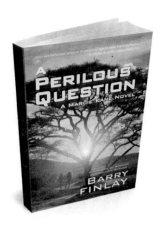

A Perilous Question: An International Thriller & Crime Novel (Marcie Kane Book 2) - While on vacation in Tanzania, Africa, Marcie's enjoyment of everything the country has to offer is shattered by one simple question posed by a teenage girl: "When are you taking me to America?" When Marcie inadvertently discovers the girls are victims of an international human trafficking ring in, of all places, her home state of Florida, her attempts to help quickly spiral out of control with terrifying consequences.

Turn the page for a preview of the second book in the *Marcie Kane Thriller Collection*.

A PERILOUS QUESTION

by

Barry Finlay

*Tanzania, Africa*

# Chapter 1

Shoni Batanga stepped back to examine her handiwork. The outline was barely visible in the indigo shadows of the room, but the moon peeking through the window cast just enough light. She inspected the profile from a distance because that's what the patrolling teacher would do. *Perfect.* Her lips turned upwards in a small smile of satisfaction. The mound in the bed, built of rolled-up bedclothes and hidden by the flimsy sheet that normally covered her as she slept, would go unnoticed until morning.

She cocked her ear to confirm the room was quiet. Shoni knew that at this time of night the fans that whirred noisily in the darkness to keep the temperature tolerable stopped automatically to preserve electricity. She cast her eye nervously at the bunk of the new girl, Aziza. In the darkness, she could barely make out the tiny girl's body curled up underneath the sheet. Even *she* seemed to be sleeping, although she had been awake many nights since she arrived. Shoni's heart was thrumming against her chest as if it were a moth trying to escape from a sealed jar. It pounded in her ears, and it occurred to her that it might be loud enough to awaken everyone in the room. She had done this before but the stakes were higher now. No matter, I'm doing the right thing, she thought.

The room was long with bunk beds aligned on both sides and a narrow space to walk between. When the head teacher, Mrs. Adimu, entered the room to check on the girls, she would be coming from the end of the room farthest from Shoni's destination. The teachers had separate quarters attached to the dormitory, and the door between the two rooms was always locked from their side to prevent the students from entering. The door leading to freedom where Shoni was headed was locked with a key from the inside. The teachers said it was so that the lock could not be picked by the male perverts that prowled from sunset to sunrise. Shoni and her classmates were told it was for their protection, but she was convinced it was to keep them from discovering what life was really like.

She crept stealthily past the rows of beds that held her sleeping classmates. Her body was tingling, her sharpened senses acutely aware of everything around her. She could hear only heavy breathing coming from all sides. She paused momentarily to listen for unwanted footfalls. Then she saw it - a movement out of the corner of her eye. A chill shimmered through her body like a sudden draft, and Shoni gasped and whipped her head around to see what had caught her attention. A scan of the room revealed nothing unusual. The door at the far end was still closed. Then she realized it was only shadow puppets dancing eerily across the wall, manipulated by the moon through the trees waving lazily in the breeze outside.

Shoni sighed quietly. As she continued, she deftly avoided the dark shapes that designated the lockers holding each girl's worldly possessions at the end of the beds. Her own extra clothing was in a small bag slung over her shoulder. She glanced at her best friend's bed located on a lower bunk and could see a mound similar to the one she had constructed - but Irene Sembaza was nowhere to be seen. Shoni's eyes narrowed and she pressed her lips together in agitation.

*I have to keep moving. Mrs. Adimu always makes her rounds later, but this is the one night she could be early.*

She arrived at the door that would take her to a better world. She sensed the fingers of freedom beckoning to her from the other side of the obstacle facing her, but a gentle twist of the door knob confirmed it was locked, as usual. Mrs. Adimu made sure the girls saw the chain with the key at the end that she carefully tucked inside the top of her dress. There was no way that anyone but The Gatekeeper, the name given to Mrs. Adimu by one of the girls, was going to access that key. But Shoni reached inside the pocket of her dress and pulled out two hairpins that had been twisted into unusual shapes by her boyfriend, Samuel.

Conflicting thoughts raced through her head.

*He's not really my boyfriend, even though we kissed a few times and I even let his hands roam over my uniform once.* She smiled inwardly. *I probably shouldn't have allowed him to do that. But there are better things awaiting me now. Oh, how I will miss all my friends, including Samuel.*

*I have to concentrate.*

Snapping back to the present, what Shoni really appreciated about Samuel right now was the trick he had shown her with the hairpins. The teachers hadn't talked about anyone picking the lock from the inside, and Samuel had shown Shoni that it was pretty simple to unlock the door so she could sneak out to see him. She had successfully used the pins twice and knew she would be able to do it again. One pin was bent at a 90 degree angle and the other had just a slight bend. As Shoni faced the door, she could barely make out the handle in the darkness. She set the small bag containing her meager belongings on the floor. Leaning forward, her eyes a few inches from her target, she fumbled with the handle until she found the tiny opening. The pin with the right angle bend easily slid into the bottom of the lock as she applied pressure. Her lips pursed as she focused on the task at hand. A drop of sweat rolled into her eyes and she blinked away the sting. She leaned back and rotated her shoulders, trying to relieve the tension. The second pin vibrated in her left hand as she leaned down again to insert it in the lock above the first.

She dropped it!

As the pin slipped from her trembling, damp hand to the floor, its fall was accompanied by an ever-increasing sick feeling descending into the pit of her stomach. The click of the pin bouncing on the concrete floor was magnified by the stillness in the room. Shoni bent down on her knees. The smooth concrete floor was cool to her touch. No pin. She brushed the floor deliberately as the last thing she wanted was to push it under the door. The hairpin moved under her sliding hand. She grasped it, straightened, and started the process again.

A hand came out of the darkness and touched her shoulder. Shoni jumped. "Kak!" She swore under her breath in Afrikaans, even though she had told herself the professional lady she was soon to become would never use bad language. In one motion, she tucked both hairpins into her pocket and whirled around to find her friend Irene looking at her sheepishly. "Sorry, I had to pee. I'm sooo excited," Irene whispered. "Have you got the door unlocked?"

"Shhh! Almost!" Shoni hissed at her friend as she listened to see if their muted utterances had awakened anyone else in the room. Everything remained still. The silence was only disturbed by the soft noises of their slumbering classmates.

Shoni wiped her clammy hands on her dress and once again fit the bent pin into the lock. As she turned it to the right and applied pressure, she inserted the second pin. It slid in easily at first, but then she felt the familiar resistance. "You have to disengage the five tumblers," Samuel had explained when he told her about the mechanics of the lock. She wiggled the second pin until she heard a click, followed by another and a third. She knew from previous experience that there would be only three clicks as two of the five tumblers had been worn down by age and use. Her breathing was labored as she leaned back, brushing against Irene who was pressed against her shoulder. Shoni noticed that

Irene had picked up the bag with her belongings. She turned the handle, pushing the door open. Hot, humid night air rushed into the room, enveloping the two girls like cellophane.

Crossing the threshold to freedom, Shoni and Irene exchanged glances, hugged briefly and ran away into the night.

## THE MARCIE KANE THRILLER COLLECTION

### (AVAILABLE INDIVIDUALLY OR AS AN E-BOOK BOXED SET)

## BOOK THREE

Remote Access: An International Political Thriller (Marcie Kane Book 3) - The president of the United States is about to impose crippling tariffs on China. A computer hacker hired by the furious Chinese regime is on a mission to stop it. The impetuous president is not listening to anyone, and especially a hacker. The hacker is equally determined not to fail. In this suspenseful cat and mouse game, Marcie unwittingly becomes involved and the stakes include national security and the life of the president.

Turn the page for a preview of the third book in the *Marcie Kane Thriller Collection*.

REMOTE ACCESS

by

Barry Finlay

# Chapter 1

The man sat hunched over his desk in the cramped space, his attention consumed by the task in front of him. He was a solitary figure in a room devoid of most of the trappings one would normally expect in an apartment, except for some heavy drapes that ensured no natural light or prying eyes could peek in. Even though his workspace was on the 8th floor, he didn't need someone with a telescope or drone observing him. He considered himself to be a very careful man and the best at his job. That's what had kept him alive until now.

Only a flickering blue light illuminated the work Yang Lee was doing. There were no pictures on the cracked and peeling walls that silently begged for some plaster and a can of paint. There was nothing except a single chair and a long desk covered in computer monitors and wireless keyboards. The room hummed with the sound of massive capacity hard drives working on shelves beside the desk. Unlike many rooms in Shanghai, this one was cooled by adequate air conditioning, more to cool the machines than for anything else. An automatic spray air freshener worked to keep pollution from seeping into the room or at least did its best to mask it when it did. The man sat on the only chair, comforted by the knowledge that the computers were doing their job, gathering data from around the world.

This was his space, the one in which he felt the most complete. His living quarters were on the other side of the city in an affluent part of Shanghai, but he spent most of his time here. He would enjoy his penthouse when he no longer relished his work.

The dancing pixels on his computer monitors illuminated Lee's raven-colored hair and handsome long, narrow face. The blue light emitted from the screens accentuated his sunken cheeks, giving him the appearance of one of the characters in *The Blair Witch Project*. But it wasn't the computer screens that occupied Lee's attention right now. His other skill had been requested, paid for and put into play. The lower half of his face was obscured by a surgical mask and his dark eyes focused on some fine dust in the bottom of the small white bowl in front of him. His lips pursed behind the mask and his eyes narrowed as he concentrated on his task. His gloved hand vigorously worked the pestle, ensuring there was nothing left of the powder he had started with except specks. The last thing he wanted to do was ingest or touch any of the dust particles he was creating. That was for someone else to do.

The powder was called aconite and it suited Lee's purposes very well. He had used it a few times because of its colorless and odorless characteristics. It was virtually untraceable.

After processing, it was often used in Chinese medicines.

Unprocessed, it was deadly.

He stopped working and leaned back in his chair to examine his handiwork. He pushed down the top of the glove on his left hand so he could see his watch.

It was time to package up his gift and present it to his next victim.

# BARRY FINLAY'S NON FICTION TITLES

**Kilimanjaro and Beyond: A Life-Changing Journey** - "Every mountaintop is within reach if you just keep on climbing." For authors Barry and Chris Finlay, this is a life-changing physical, mental and spiritual adventure. Follow along as the pair strive to climb one of the World's Seven Summits, meet the children who will benefit from their fundraising, and come to an understanding that one or two people really can make a difference. It is a journey that leaves the two with the lasting impression that nothing is more satisfying than reaching a goal and giving others the opportunity to achieve theirs.

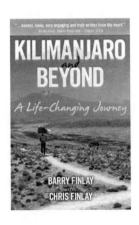

**I Guess We Missed the Boat** - When eight intrepid seniors, brought together by marriage and with retirement in common, sit reminiscing about their travel experiences, the memory banks open and hilarious events start to spill out. Cowboy Ron, Ed the Negotiator, Joke-a Minute Jim and Practical Carol are part of the motley crew comprising the author's contingent of six in-laws. Each, at one time or another, has a role to play in the events that occur on their travels. Reviewers have termed it "laugh out loud hilarious", "an exhilarating read" and "definitely a ride worth taking."

BUY ONLINE OR AT YOUR FAVORITE BOOK STORE

www.barry-finlay.com